Lew M. Miller

The Last of the House of Jeffreys

A Drama in Five Acts

Lew M. Miller

The Last of the House of Jeffreys
A Drama in Five Acts

ISBN/EAN: 9783337343224

Printed in Europe, USA, Canada, Australia, Japan

Cover: Foto ©Andreas Hilbeck / pixelio.de

More available books at **www.hansebooks.com**

THE LAST

OF THE

HOUSE OF JEFFREYS;

A DRAMA IN FIVE ACTS.

By LEW. M. MILLER.

~~~~~~~~~~~~~~~~~~

MT. CLEMENS, MICH.:
PRESS BOOK AND JOB PRINT.
1878.

DRAMATIS PERSONÆ.

SAMUEL JEFFREYS,..An elderly gentleman of wealth.
RICHARD JEFFREYS...His nephew.
GEORGE HALLIDAY..His confidential companion.
EDWARD JENNISON.. ......A young lawyer.
JACK HOTALING...A villain.
BENJAMIN FRANKLIN PYMAKER.......................................A tramp printer.
MICHEL O'BLARNEY..Keeper of a low groggery.
POMPEY........... ....Jeffreys' colored servant.
NELLIE HALLIDAY............. ....Halliday's daughter.
MISS ANGELINA WYCKOFF...A stylish maiden lady.
MRS. HOUGH........... ....An old housekeeper.
MRS. O'BLARNEY........... ....An apple woman.

Costume—MODERN.

Entered according to act of Congress, in the year 1878,
By LEW. M. MILLER,
In the office of the Librarian of Congress, at Washington.

THE LAST OF THE HOUSE OF JEFFREYS.

ACT I.

SCENE.—JEFFREYS' *room; door at back leading to main part of house; door* L. H. *leading to hall; writing desk* R. H., *safe and table with call-bell* L. H. JEFFREYS *seated right of table and* HALLIDAY *left.*

Hall. What are you thinking about so intently, Mr. Jeffreys?—you seem troubled this morning.

Jeff. Yes, I am troubled—I have been recalling the past.

Hall. And does the recollection of the past bring you naught but sorrow?.

Jeff. Naught but sorrow.

Hall. It is not so with me. I dearly love to recall the happy scenes of my early life. To me they are like pictures, but far more fascinating than those master-pieces which adorn the walls of wealth and luxury.

Jeff. You are very enthusiastic, Halliday, and I would to God that the same enthusiasm might pervade my breast. But you seem to forget the black cloud which has darkened my whole life and still casts its baneful shadow over every picture—however fair—that Memory may paint for me.

Hall. Can you recall no pleasures unalloyed by your great affliction?

Jeff. [*Rising.*] No, no, Halliday, not one. Every retrospective view of my life but serves to remind me how that cloud, which shadowed the very dayspring of my existence, has grown blacker and

2 THE LAST OF THE HOUSE OF JEFFREYS.

Hall. [*Rising. Aside.*] I must not allow him to continue in this despondent mood. [*Aloud.*] But, Mr. Jeffreys, the blacker the cloud, the brighter is its "silver lining."

Jeff. [*Impatiently.*] Yes, yes; you have told me that again and again. It is doubtless true, and will bear repeating an indefinite number of times; but the "silver lining" is turned toward the sun and not toward me.

Hall. Trust in the Almighty. He will yet turn toward you the "silver lining" of that threatening cloud.

Jeff. [*Excitedly.*] Will the Lord reverse the order of nature for my sake? Will he turn the "silver lining" of that cloud away from the sun and toward the earth, simply that it may illumine the last few hours of a life, which he has allowed to be shadowed so long? Generations have come and gone since that curse fell upon our family, and in every generation has the fated first-born fallen beneath its withering blight. I have prayed that the curse might be removed and that, when my time shall come, I may be permitted to die like a Christian and not like a throttled dog. But no, no; it cannot be removed. [*Sinks into chair.*

[*Knock heard* L.]

Hall. Compose yourself, Mr. Jeffreys—someone raps.

Jeff. I presume it is my nephew. If so, you may retire, as I wish to see him alone.

HALLIDAY *admits* RICHARD *and exit* L.

Jeff. Good morning, Richard—what is it you wish?

Rich. I have come for some money—I need some very much.

Jeff. Need some, Richard? I gave you $500 last week. Have you none of it left?

Rich. [*Aside.*] I wonder what's come over the old fool now - he never hesitated like this before. [*Aloud.*] Not a cent of it left and I need $200 more. Will you let me have it? yes or no.

Jeff. I will think of it, Richard.

Rich. Think of it! You never stopped to think of it before, when I asked you for so trifling a sum.

Jeff. I cannot let you have that sum, unless you tell me why you want it.

Rich. You have never required this of me before and it is too late to begin now. I will not submit.

Jeff. [*Rising.*] Richard, I fear that I have already given you too much of my money to be squandered. [RICHARD *scowls.*] Do not scowl upon me, Richard. I use plain language, but the case demands it. I implore you to hear the truth and be warned in time. Unless you reform your ways, you will soon be a disgrace to that family, whose only hope of honor and existence lies in you.

Rich. I did not come here to be insulted nor to hear a sermon. Will you give me the money?

Jeff. I cannot, Richard, though it grieves me to say so.

Rich. Then I have no further business with you at present. [*As* RICHARD *retires,* JEFFREYS *sinks into chair.* RICHARD *turns and scowls at his uncle. Aside.*] Curses on his miserly soul—but I'll find a way to make him disgorge.   [*Exit* L.

Jeff. His conduct cuts me to the heart. He resists all counsel, all warning, all entreaty. It seems as if every evil trait, which disfigured the character of old Benjamin Jeffreys, were fated to re-appear in him. And when I think that the very fate of our house depends upon him, it almost crazes me. One branch of the family becomes extinct in me, but Richard might continue the family name, freed from that curse which has blighted the lineal descent.

Enter HALLIDAY.

Hall. It is a lovely morning, Mr. Jeffreys—would you like to take a drive?

Jeff. Nothing could please me more.   [*Rings bell.*

Enter POMPEY L.

Pomp. Did wun ob you respected gemlums manipulate dat ar bell?

Jeff. Yes, Pompey, I summoned you. Go and tell James to drive the carriage around to the front door.

Pomp. Yes, sah.   [*Exit* L.

Jeff Halliday, I have revealed more of myself to you this morning, than I have before in all the ten years we have lived so intimately together. But, of late, I have felt more and more in need of a confidant. I could not turn to Richard, so I have turned to you.

Hall. And I will inviolably keep any confidence you may repose in me.

Jeff. Bless you for that, Halliday.

Hall. I am so deeply indebted to you that it would be the basest perfidy in me to do otherwise. You found me financially ruined at too late a period in life to start anew, and you offered my daughter and myself a home. How can I ever repay you?

Jeff. You have been amply repaying me all this time by your companionship. All accounts between us are balanced.

Enter POMPEY L

Pomp. De carrige am ready, sah.

Jeff. Well, Pompey, go and tell Mrs. Hough that I am going out and I want my room swept while I am gone.

Pomp. Yes, sah.   [*Exit* L.

Jeff. Now, Halliday, never let me hear you say anything more about repayment. It is I, who am indebted to you, for your kindness and forbearance.   [*Exeunt* L.

[*Enter* NELLIE, *followed by* MRS. HOUGH *carrying broom, dust-pan and brush,* C. E.

Nel. Now we'll give Mr. Jeffreys' room a good cleaning.

[MRS. HOUGH *sweeps and* NELLIE *re-arranges furniture,&c.*]

Mrs. H. I do wonder how on arth Mr. Jeffreys manages to litter up his room so. [*Sweeps around desk.*] If I kep' my part of the house a lookin' so, I'd be 'shamed to see cumpny, so I would, an' I'd be discharged in a minnit. [*Rings bell. Enter* POMPEY.] Pompey, come an' help me move this desk.

[*They move desk and* POMPEY *sets it down on his toe, yells, jumps back against* MRS. HOUGH, *who hits him with broom.*

Nel. Do be quiet, Pompey.
Pomp. Be quiet wid a two-ton desk on my corns? [*Holding up foot.*] Corns grows mighty big an' tender in tight boots like dat.
Mrs. H. Why don't he have this room swep' out off"ner? [*Sweeps around safe.*] Here, Pompey, move this safe.
Pomp. [*Pushing against safe with head and hands.*] No go, Missis Hough—can't budge it.
Mrs. H. Never mind then. Jest about twice a week Mr. Jeffreys sends for me to sweep out his room, an' them's the only times I sees the inside of it.
Nel. Mr. Jeffreys doesn't like to have women in his room much.
Pomp. [*Aside.*] Golly! I'd like to hab my room full ob 'em.
Mrs. H. Pompey, come here an' hold this dust pan. I do declare, I never got sich a heep o' dirt out o' one room afore in all my life. [*Gives broom a spiteful push, throwing dust into* POMPEY'S *face.* POMPEY *makes up face and blows nose.*] It makes me 'shamed, so it does. My old mother used to say that a good house-keeper's broom never caught much dirt. [*Throws more dust into* POMPEY'S *face.*
Pomp. [*Blowing nose.*] Den dis niggah's nose ain't a good housekeepah's broom, fur it cotched a heep o' dirt dat time.
Mrs. H. [*Pointing to pan.*] Look a' that, will ye—I've a good mind to hav Pompey take it out in the wheel barrow.
Nel. [*Laughing.*] Don't, Mrs. Hough—the wheel would leave more dirt than the barrow would carry out.

(POMPEY *carries dust-pan out* C. E. *and returns.*)

Mrs H. (*Dusting.*) Well, Mr. Jeffreys ought to hav a better opinion of us women, anyhow—smart a man as he is. How'd the world git along 'thout us women, I'd like to know?
Nel. I give it up. Perhaps the men wouldn't have so much to quarrel about, though.
Mrs. H. They'd quarrel a big sight more—they'd soon be a pack o' howlin' an' ravin' wild beasts, if it wasn't fur the humanizin' influence of us women.
Pomp. (*Aside.*) Wonder how many she's humanized.

[*Pompey goes behind* Mrs. Hough *and gesticulates comically, while she puts arms akimbo and continues.*

Mrs. H. Didn't the Lord make Eve for Adam right off, 'cause He knew it wouldn't a been two weeks afore Adam'd a been a roarin' an' ravin' an' tearin' round Eden, a killin' an' destroyin' everything like a savage lion ? The Lord knew best, an' so men an' women'd ought to go together through this world. Them's my sentiments !

Pomp. [*With great delight.*] Selah !

Mrs. H. [*Driving him out* L. *with broom.*] Sass me agin, will ye.

Nel. Well, Mrs. Hough, when Mr. Jeffreys returns, he'll own at once that much of man's happiness in this world is due to woman's gentler influence.

Mrs. H. If he don't hav his room swep' out off"ner'n twice a week, it'll take something stronger'n "woman's gentler influence" to start the dirt.

Nel. You may go now, Mrs. Hough. [*Exit* Mrs. Hough, c. e., *with broom and dust-brush.*] I know Mr. Jeffreys will like this. [*Looking about.*] His life is a sad one and I will do what little I can to brighten it. What else can I do for him here? Oh, yes ! I'll take that pitcher out and have Mrs. Hough wash it. [*Exit* c. e. *singing.*

Enter RICHARD L. E.

Rich. [*Looking about.*] I am sure I heard Nellie singing in here, and yet I do not see her. She must have stepped out just as I came in. What a lovely creature she is ! I'm bound to have her, though she does n't seem to take to me very fondly. Love her ? As well as I can love any woman. I look upon women only as the playthings of this life, not as its serious concerns. When they are worn and faded, cast them off an'd get new ones. Now, Nellie is young, handsome and talented, and she'll make a magnificent mistress for this old mansion, when it is mine—and it soon will be, together with the accumulated wealth of the House of Jeffreys. How I long to get my hands upon it. [NELLIE *sings outside.*] But I hear Nellie singing. She must be coming back. Now, Richard Jeffreys, be a model lover—all smiles and honeyed words. [*Enter* NELLIE c. e., *with pitcher.*] Good morning, Nellie.

Nel. [*Starting, but recovering herself and setting down pitcher.*] Good morning, Mr. Jeffreys.

Rich. What have you been doing to make you look so bright this morning?

Nel. Simply trying to make your uncle's room look a little more cosy.

Rich. Ah ! then it is the kindness of your heart that I see reflected in your face.

Nel. [*Coolly.*] I was not aware, Mr. Jeffreys, that my face presented any unusual appearance, this morning.

Rich. You always look pretty, Nellie, but I thought you were looking unusually handsome this morning. But why do you call me

"Mr. Jeffreys," Nellie?—it used to be "Richard," or "Dick," until recently.

Nel. As long as we were children together, and before you persisted in forcing your professions of love upon me, I called you by those names, but now I prefer to address you as "Mr. Jeffreys."

Rich. And is there no hope for me, Nellie?

Nel. None whatever.

Rich. And must I give you up? [*Kneeling.*] I swear that I love you devotedly—as I never can love another—with as pure an affection as man ever bore to woman. Then why so cold? I am ruined if you drive me to despair.

Nel. Arise, Richard Jeffreys your pleading is in vain. I have given you my answer already.

Rich. Hear me once more, Nellie. We have played together as little children—we have grown into womanhood and manhood together. Just so has my love grown from a childish affection to a manly passion. I know not how to live without you.

Nel. Cease your pitiful teasing. [RICHARD *springs to his feet.*] Do not lower your manhood by indulging in it longer. Change your ways, Richard Jeffreys, before you expect any pure woman to accept your love.

Rich. Woman! I know the secret of all this. You prefer the love of Edward Jennison, who is not worth a picayune, but who hopes to win you and induce my uncle to leave you some of his vast wealth.

Nel. It is cowardly to speak thus of a man who is not present to defend himself. I will not hear you. Leave this room instantly or I will.

Rich. I go, but this is not the last, Miss Halliday.   [*Exit* L.

Nel. What have I done? What have I said? Oh! I have been so tormented by his continued professions of love, that I spoke before I thought. I cannot accept him as a lover, yet I fear him as an enemy. What shall I do?   [*Sinks into chair.*

Enter POMPEY L., *admitting* JENNISON.

Pomp. Mr. Jeffreys am not heah jis now, but jis you took a chah, Mr. Jennison, an' wait till he comes back.

Jen. I will do so, Pompey. [*Seeing* NELLIE.] Why, Nellie, you here?

Pomp. [*Aside.*] Guess he don' care if Mr. Jeffreys don' come back 'fore suppah time.   [*Exit.*

Nel. Oh, Edward! I am so glad to see you.

Jen. Are you, pet? [*Kisses her.*] How long have you been keeping office for Mr. Jeffreys?

Nel. Oh, Mrs. Hough and I have been cleaning up Mr. Jeffreys' room. Doesn't it look nice?

Jen. It does but you're the only nice thing I can see just at present, Nellie.

Nel. Come, sir, no flattery.

Jen. Well, Nellie, I have some good news for you.

Nel. What is it ?—I'm all curiosity.

Jen. Your father has given his consent.

Nel. To what, Edward ?

Jen. To our marriage. Now isn't that good news ?

Nel. I don't know. That depends upon how well you'll "love, honor and *obey*" me.

Jen. Oh, you little humbug, we'll be married by a Justice of the Peace and skip all that nonsense. But when shall it be, Nellie ?

Nel. Don't ask me now, Edward. I cannot leave here yet. Mr. Jeffreys wouldn't have anyone to manage his household, if I left. But when did you see father ?

Jen. Yesterday. Now I shall be jealous of Mr. Jeffreys, if you keep me waiting long on his account—you know he is a bachelor.

Nel. Yes—and a rich one, too.

Jen. N w I am jealous.

Nel. Hark ! I hear them coming in the hall. You sit down and I'll run out. [*Exit* C. E., JENNISON *following her to door.*

Enter JEFFREYS *and* HALLIDAY L.

Jeff. Why, good morning, Mr. Jennison—have you waited long ? I am sorry I was not in.

Jen. I have not waited long. Mr. Jeffreys Good morning, Mr. Halliday.

Hal. Good morning.

Jeff. Be seated, please. [*They sit.*] Have you any business with me, Mr. Jennison ?

Jen. I have called to ask for your subscription to the new bridge.

Jeff. You shall have it—$100, I believe. [*Goes to desk and fills out check.*] Is the bridge well under way ?

Jen. Yes, and it will be a fine one.

Jeff. I'll drive around and see it soon. [*Giving check.*] There's my check.

Jen. [*Rising.*] Thank you. Good morning, gentlemen.

Jeff. Good morning.

Hal. Good morning. [*Exit* JENNISON.] There goes a specimen of true manhood, Mr. Jeffreys.

Jeff. Yes—would to God that my nephew were like him. He has been waiting on Nellie of late, hasn't he ?

Hal. He has, and yesterday he asked my consent to their future marriage.

Jeff. You gave it, of course.

Hal. Certainly.

Jeff. There was a time when I thought of such a union between Nellie and Richard. But that is impossible now—there can be no union of Virtue and Vice. Halliday, I have been deeply interest ed in Nellie for some time. I have watched her develop from girl- hood into womanhood, unfolding new charms every day. Though I have avoided her, as I have avoided all women for many years, yet I could not wholly ignore her. She reminds me of another maiden, whom I loved years ago—but you look surprised, Halliday, —you little thought I ever took more than a passing interes. in any woman.

Hal. You are right—I little thought so.

Jeff. In early manhood I determined to live a single life, that I might put an end to that awful curse which rests upon our house. I afterward met a lovely girl. I loved her with all the ardor of impassioned manhood. She returned my love. In my delirium of joy I forgot my terrible fate, until one day it flashed across my mind and sent me shrieking from her sight. I have never seen her since. [*Clasps hands beseechingly.*] Oh! Helen, Helen Partington—

Hal. [*Springing up*] Helen Partington, did you say?

Jeff. Yes, did you know her?

Hal. Helen Partington of Ashville?

Jeff. The same—what was she to you?

Hal. She was my wife.

Jeff. [*Springing up.*] Your wife?

Hal. Yes.

Jeff. And the mother of Nellie Halliday?

Hal. The mother of my daughter.

[*They look at each other in mute astonishment.*]

Jeff. I can scarcely comprehend it—and yet I might have known it, for Nellie resembles her mother so closely. [*Resuming his seat.*] But, come, Halliday, tell me all about it.

Hal. [*Taking a seat nearer* JEFFREYS.] I came to Ashville—it must have been some time after you left—and formed the acquaintance of Helen's parents. They became very much attached to me and, before long, I was a frequent visitor at their house. I was at that time about forty years of age, and had determined to quit my roving way of life and settle down. Helen's beauty and sweet disposition attracted me and I asked her to be my wife. She consented—in compliance with the urgent request of her parents, as I afterward learned—and we were married. But some great grief had broken her heart—

Jeff. May God forgive me!

Hal. And she gradually faded, until, scarcely two years after our marriage, she was borne to her grave. But she left me another Helen—my darling Nellie—and I would that, when I am taken away, I might leave her more safely insured against the perils of this life.

Jeff. Fear not, Halliday—she shall be provided for. The daughter of Helen Partington shall never want, if I can prevent it.

Hal. But, Mr. Jeffreys, we are no fortune hunters—

Jeff. Say no more, Halliday—my resolution is taken. Naught can shake it. I have long known that Richard is not a fit person to control my property after I am gone, and the thought of making some other disposition of that property is not a new one to me.

[RICHARD *opens* C. E. *as if to enter, but, hearing the next sentence, stops and listens.*] I shall make my will this afternoon.

Rich. [*Aside.*] His will? I must learn its contents. Go on, uncle—I'm all attention.

Jeff. I shall give the bulk of my property to Nellie, leaving Richard only $10,000. That is enough for him, if he uses it properly, and too much, if he squanders it. The contents of the will shall remain a secret between us two, until I am gone

Rich. [*Aside.*] That's a lie. [*Exit*

Hal. I shall consider the secret a sacred trust.

Jeff. But, Halliday, I want to see Nellie—see her now. Bid her come hither. [HALLIDAY *rings bell.*

Enter POMPEY L.

Pomp. Did you ring, sah?

Hal. Do you know where Miss Nellie is?

Pomp I seed her in de kitchum 'bout fifteen minnits ago, an' she was a gibin' de ole housekeepah de ordahs fur dinnah. Glory! didn't it sound salubrious in dis niggah's eahs to heah her enumerate de multinumerous kinds ob hash—

Hal. That will do, Pompey. Go and tell Miss Nellie that Mr. Jeffreys would like to see her. [*Exit* POMPEY.

Jeff. Ten long and weary years in the same house with my Helen's child, and I did not mistrust the relationship! How strange it all seems! Truth is indeed stranger than fiction!

Enter POMPEY L.

Pomp. She'll be heah immejiously. [*Sees her.*] Oh, heah she am now.

Enter NELLIE L.

Nel. Did you send for me, Mr. Jeffreys?

[JEFFREYS *looks at her intently, but does not reply. She is startled at his strange appearance, but is re-assured by a sign from her father, who rises.* POMPEY *goes around behind* NELLIE, *looking at her admiringly.*

Pomp. Ain't she pooty? If she was only sixteen shades blacker, she'd be as lubly as Wenus, an' I'd ax her to be Mrs. Pompey Cæsar Augustus George Washington Browne—I would.

[JEFFREYS *rises and approaches* NELLIE *slowly, as if fearful of frightening away some pleasing object. She is again re-assured by her father.* POMPEY *sees the strange appearance of* JEFFREYS *and runs out.*

Jeff. [*Slowly approaching.*] My Helen—my own Helen? Or is it but a cruel vision sent to torment me? [*Touching her forehead.*] Yes, 'tis she—'tis Helen Partington!—this is her forehead, her chin—these are her eyes, her lips. My Helen has come to me again—yet she cannot sta —no, no!—she must soor return—no other angel could fill her place amid the Heavenly Hosts. [*Overcome by feelings and trembling violently.* HALLIDAY *wheels up a chair and helps him into it. After a moment's silence* JEFFREYS *appears to notice* NELLIE *for the first time.*] Nellie, come here. [*She approaches and he takes her hands.*] I have been living in the past. Your striking resemblance to your mother reminds me of her.

Nel. You knew her, then?

Jeff. I loved her, Nellie, yet I wronged her. I won her love and then abandoned her. Can you forgive me for so wronging her?

Nel. I know that she would forgive you, if she were here—and, surely, I can forgive you.

Jeff. Bless you, Nellie—you have your mother's own kind heart. Your father will explain all, when I am gone.

Hal. I fear that she will grow very impatient, if she waits until then, Mr. Jeffreys.

Jeff. No, no; it will not be long—I feel that the end is near. [*Rising.*] Nellie, receive the blessing of an old man, who has been crushed to earth for the sins of another. [*She kneels.*] God bless you, Nellie. May the future ever brighten before you.

TABLEAU.

END OF ACT I.

ACT II.

SCENE 1.—*Open space in the woods; a log* L. H. *and a rock* R. H.— *Early evening.*

Enter PYMAKER L., *shabbily dressed and with one coat-tail torn off.*

i y. [*Singing.*] "Tramp, tramp, tramp, the boys are marching," Well, let 'em march – I'll go no farther. Here I'll rest. This luxuriant grass shall be my couch, and

> "The spacious firmament on high,
> With all the blue, ethereal sky,"

shall be my bed-quilt. But I'll have my supper, ere I "wrap the drapery of my couch about me and lie down to pleasant dreams." [*Feels for eatables and misses one tail of his coat.*] Ha-ha-ha! "Thereby hangs a tale." Yea, verily; "I could a tale unfold" in reference to that "bloody chasm." Jupiter! but it was a narrow escape. The bull-dog didn't get me, but he sampled my coat-tail, as I sped through the gate. [*Finds a bone in pocket of the other tail.*] Ha! a streak of luck! the savage bull-pup didn't get this tail. Here are the remains of my dinner. Now for the banquet. [*Sits down on log.*] Let me see if I've got a knife. [*Feels in pocket and takes out a spoon.*] A spoon! solid silver, too! What are these initials?—"J. G. W."—oh! that reminds me. Miss Angelina Wyckoff's cook gave me a lunch in the kitchen, the other day, and I was just getting ready to give my stomach a grand surprise party, when in came Miss Angelina—the angelic creature—and hustled me out doors in a jiffy. So I took the spoon in lieu of the lunch. [*Lays spoon in his lap and searches for knife.*] No knife? Well, I'll use my composing rule—'twon't be the first time. [*Picks bone.*] I ran across the village marshal to-day. He was going to arrest me as a vagrant with no "visible means of support." I showed him my composing rule and told him I was a first-class printer and "belonged to the Union." Then he was mad. He thought I was going to start a new paper in town, and he kicked me clear out of the corporation, advising me never to set foot in it again. I think I shall take his advice. [*Throws away bone.*] There, I feel better. Now I'll take a smoke before I retire. [*Fills an old clay pipe, lights it, takes a few whiffs and starts up, dropping spoon.*] What's that?   [*Looking toward* L. H. *and listening.*

> ——"Is't but the wind,
> Or the car rattling o'er the stony street?"

No, it's some one coming—I'll not wait to see whether he has the countersign.   [*Gets behind rock.*

Enter HOTALING L. H.

Hot [*Looking around.*] He's not here yet. Well, I'll wait, but if he fails me he'll rue it. [*Sits down on log*] What's that? [*Picks up spoon.*] A spoon? Wonder how it came here--lost by some pic-nic party, I presume. I'll stow it away for future inspection. [*Puts it into pocket.*] There, I'm a spoon ahead.

Py. [*Peering cautiously.*] And I'm a spoon behind.

Hot. It's getting dark and Jeffreys ought to be here by this time. Curse the fool! how long must I wait for him? [*Takes out flask and drinks.*

Py. Ha! he drinks! That's one bond of sympathy between us. [HOTALING *takes out a plug of tobacco and bites off a piece.*] He chews! —bond of sympathy No. 2. He must be a brother printer.

Hot. [*Seeing* RICHARD *coming* L. *Rising.*] Hello! Jeffreys. you are rather late.

Py. [*Crouching low.*] There's a pair of 'em. I'll vegetate here in the shade—it's so refreshing.

Enter RICHARD.

Rich. Yes, somewhat late—I've been detained. Have you waited long?

Hot. Long? That's cool. I began to think you were going to fail me. If you had—

Rich. Make no threats, Hotaling. I'm not easily frightened, as you well know.

Hot. [*Surlily.*] Well, have you brought the money?

Rich. No.

Hot. What! would you play me false? Richard Jeffreys, I'll not be trifled with.   [*Draws knife.*

Rich. [*Drawing revolver.*] Be calm, Jack. I'm not afraid of your knife when my little pet is near. She never failed me yet. She speaks but one word, and that word is "DEATH." *[*Aiming it.*

Py. Oh, Lord! I wish I was out of this.

Hot. [*Starting back in fear, but recovering composure in a moment.*] I forgot myself, Jeffreys. We must not quarrel—we know each oth-er too well to be enemies.   [*They put up weapons.*

Rich. You're rational now.

Py. The storm is o'er—fair weather again.

Hot. But why is the money not forthcoming? It's an honest debt you owe me, and you promised to settle it this evening.

Rich. An honest debt? Ha-ha-ha-a-a-a! that's too good! Real-ly, Hotaling, you're quite a joker. Ha-ha-a-a—

Hot. [*Nettled.*] What do you mean?

Rich. Mean?—that you cheated like a thief, when you won that money. Is my meaning plain now?

Hot. Do you mean to insult me?

Py. Another typhoon!

Rich. Restrain yourself. My little pet is uneasy in her close quarters.   [*Putting hand on revolver pocket.*

Hot. Do you intend to "squeal" now?

Rich. No, I intend to pay the debt like a gentleman.

Py. Blue sky once more,

Hot. Then why in h—l did'nt you bring the money? You know I want to leave this vicinity as soon as possible—it's getting too hot for me here.

Rich. Really! What part of the country is going to be favored with your valuable presence?

Hot. That's none of your d—n business.

Rich. Well, sit down on this log and I'll explain. [*They sit.*] I couldn't raise that sum. I asked my uncle for the money and he preached me a sermon instead of shelling out—curse the old fool!

Hot. Well, how does that help my case? I must have the money, for I've got to leave here at once.

Py. Bond of sympathy No. 3. Villain No. 1 has got to "skin out" and so have I.

Rich. [*After a moment's reflection.*] How much longer could you stay hereabouts for an adequate consideration?

Hot. Consideration? What consideration can you give me for running that risk, if you can't raise enough to pay me what you owe me already?

Rich. I might find you a job, if you would accept.

Hot. Accept? Did you ever know me to refuse any job that offered good inducements? Besides, I am desperate now and I must have money. So out with it!

Rich. [*Drawing closer to* HOTALING.] If it wasn't for my uncle, I might have money enough to settle all my debts and live like a gentleman.

Py. [*Trying to hear.*] A little louder, Villain No. 2.

Hot. [*Thoughtfully.*] Ah!—um—I "twig." A sudden death and a convenient funeral would afford great relief to your embarrassed finances.

Rich. Just so.

Hot. Risky business,

Rich. Good pay.

Hot. How much?

Rich. $1,000.

Hot. Bah! a mere bagatelle.

Rich. $2,000—besides the $200 I owe you now.

Py. [*In an agony of curiosity.*] Do speak a little louder.

Hot. [*Thoughtfully.*] $2,200—nice little sum to emigrate with—agreed! What's your plan of operations?

Rich. Can you play the part of a devil?

Hot. [*Laughing.*] I've played the devil in the community ever since I left my swaddling clothes. Yes, I think I could—but do you want me to scare the old fool to death?

Rich. Not exactly. My uncle is the victim of a strange delusion—

Hot. Yes, I've heard of it—he thinks the devil is coming after him some night.

Rich. He believes that a remote ancestor of his, named Benjamin

Jeffreys, once entered into a solemn compact with the devil, the forfeit of which was to be the first-born of every succeeding generation. Old Benjamin, who was never known to keep faith with his fellow man, played one of his customary tricks on the devil—

Hot. And the devil foreclosed.

Rich. Exactly. Now, my uncle declares that his father, his grandfather and his great-grandfather all died mysteriously, when no one was near to observe the cause or manner of their death, but in every case the evidence was plain of death by strangulation. He is ever on the look-out for the devil, and whenever that interesting personage puts in an appearance, my uncle will undoubtedly resign himself to his fate. You understand?

Hot. Yes; you want me to be that "interesting personage."

Rich. My uncle has never married and his death, as he declares, will rid the family of that horrid curse—

Hot. And you of the curse of poverty.

Rich. I admire your acuteness.

Py. [*Moving uneasily.*] This seat might be softer.

Hot. And this awful curse does not affect the collateral branch of the family?

Rich. No.

Hot. You think that's lucky for you, don't you?

Rich. Yes, rather.

Hot. But that doesn't trouble the devil much.

Rich. Why so?

Hot. Oh, he's sure of the collateral branch.

Rich. [*Starting up and putting hand on revolver.*] Do you dare—

Hot. Be calm, Jeffreys. Neither one of us must die until this awful curse is removed from the House of Jeffreys, you know.

Py. This play might be highly entertaining, if I could only hear it.

Rich. [*Sitting down again.*] My uncle's regular attendant, who has slept in the same room with him for several years, will be away to-morrow night. No one will be with him except his colored servant, who is an arrant coward and he will be so badly frightened at the appearance of the devil, that he will be easily managed. But you had better take your trusty knife along as a matter of precaution.

Hot. That all sounds very fine—but what if anything should happen? I'd make a pretty looking corpse dressed up in that kind of toggery, now wouldn't I? My own mother wouldn't know me—and then, just imagine what a figure I'd cut in the *Police Gazette*—ahem! —"Jack Hotaling as he appeared in the *role* of the Devil—One Night Only!!"

Rich. But nothing will happen—I'll see that there is no interruption. But one thing more. In the safe that stands in my uncle's office is his will. I will teach you the combination. Open the safe, find the will, lock the safe carefully behind you and bring me that will.

Hot. Oh, ho! that's another thing altogether. If I bring you that will, you ought to make the consideration a clean $2,500.

Rich. I will. We understand each other now?

Hot. Perfectly.

Rich. [*Rising.*] Then good night—I'll see you again. [*Exit* L.

Py. Now I'll get a chance to stretch my legs.

Hot. [*Rising.*] Jack Hotaling, you're in luck! $2,500 to begin operations with in the Black Hills—all for choking off an old man who expects the devil after him soon, anyway. [*Exit* L.

Py. [*Coming out cautiously.*] "Now is the winter of our discontent made glorious summer." Those two villains are up to some mischief, I know, but my information is altogether too limited to warrant me in risking my precious person back in the village to interfere with their plans. Nor do I think so much of this spot for a bed-room, after all. I'll meander. Hello! there's the moon.

[*Exit* R . *singing.*

> The silvery moon, with her kerosene lamp,
> Illumines the path of the weary tramp.

SCENE II.—*A street.*

Enter RICHARD R., *walking rapidly.*

Rich. I must hasten—the time is short and many things must be carefully arranged before to-night. [*Enter* JENNISON L. *They meet.* RICHARD *stops and scowls.*] Edward Jennison, you are in my way.

Jen. Do you speak literally or figuratively, Mr. Jeffreys? If literally, just step to the right. I will do the same and then we can pass without a collision. If you speak figuratively, explain yourself.

Rich. None of your lawyer's quibbles here, sir. You are in my way.

Jen. When I am convinced that I have trespassed on your rights or privileges, I am willing to withdraw—but not before.

Rich. I have a faculty of clearing my way before me.

Jen. The best way of clearing your pathway of my presence is to be civil and convince me that I am wrongfully in it. Until you can do so, I decline to yield in any way, sir. Good morning. [*Crosses.*

Rich. You love Nellie Halliday.

Jen. And if I do, I have no apology to make to you, sir.

Rich. I ask no apology. I simply wished to warn you not to cross my path again. Do you understand?

Jen. Whenever Nellie Halliday shall have chosen you, in preference to me, then will your pathway be relieved of my presence.

Rich. Meanwhile, it will be well for you not to darken my house with your presence.

Jen. *Your* house? I was not aware that you owned any. Have you purchased one recently, in view of a possible marriage with

Miss Halliday?

Rich. [*Aside.*] Curse him for his impudence! [*Aloud.*] I meant my uncle's house, of course.

Jen. Well, what right have you to forbid my entering your uncle's house?

Rich. I may have a right sooner than you expect.

Jen. When you have such right, I will ask your consent to call. Until then, adieu.   [*Exit* R.

Rich. Curse him for his impudence and obstinacy! I may have to give Hotaling another job. But here comes Miss Wyckoff. I'll await her. [*Enter* Miss Wyckoff.] Good morning, Miss Wyckoff.

Miss W. Good morning, Mr. Jeffreys.

Rich. You are out shopping rather early this morning.

Miss W. Rather early, perhaps—but I had several errands to do, so I told John to get out the carriage and drive me down.

Rich. Where is your carriage now?

Miss W. Just around the corner, waiting while I step into my milliner's.

Rich. Well, I'll not detain you long. How is your suit progressing with Mr. Jennison?

Miss W. Oh, finely! He thinks I have a sure case and he will notice it for trial at the next term. Mr. Jennison is a smart lawyer.

Rich. Jennison is a fool!

Miss W. Well, that doesn't seem to hurt him any as a lawyer. At any rate he's a shrewd one.

Rich. Well, Miss Wyckoff, I really didn't have any reference to your *lawsuit*, when I asked that question. I meant another kind of suit, altogether—one in which Cupid is popularly supposed to be the chief mediator.

Miss W. What do you mean, sir, by asking me so impertinent a question?

Rich. Now don't be so indignant about it, Miss Wyckoff. Every one knows how hard you are trying to catch the wily lawyer with the bait of a good fat lawsuit.

Miss W. This impudence is unbearable, sir. Let me pass.

Rich. Certainly. [*She crosses.*] But wait a moment, Miss Wyckoff. I have something interesting to tell you. [*She stops. Aside.*] I thought her curiosity would overcome her indignation. [*Aloud.*] Mr. Jennison is becoming very much interested in Nellie Halliday.

Miss W. What! that doll-faced thing?

Rich. [*Aside.*] You can always rely upon a woman's jealousy to liberate the feline. [*Aloud.*] My means of observation are good and I give it to you as my candid opinion, that they will soon be engaged, if they are not already.

Miss W. I took Mr. Jennison to be a man of sense.

Rich. It was only a moment since that I remarked that he was not.

Miss W. Does *she* love *him?*

Rich. Unfortunately for *me*, she does.

Miss W. Ah! then *you* are interested, too.

Rich. I am. [*Approaching her.*] Now, Miss Wyckoff, since we are both in the same foundering boat, it only remains for us to help each other out of difficulty, or go down in one loving embrace together.

Miss W. I prefer the former alternative, sir.

Rich. So do I—vastly—remarkable unanimity of opinion, isn't it?

Miss W. Well, no more of this in the street. I must go now.

Rich. We'll meet again, Miss Wyckoff?

Miss W. At another time and place. Good morning.

Rich. Good morning. [*Exit* Miss W. R.] If I can only manage Nellie, as well as I can that delectable piece of dry goods, all will be well. Oh, how I love to play with the dear creatures—manage them as I would a set of chess-men.   [*Exit* L.

SCENE III.—*Back room in* JEFFREYS' *house.*

Enter MRS. HOUGH *and* POMPEY, L. H., *bringing table, with ironing board, flat-irons and basket of clothes.*

Mrs. H. I declare—it was so hot in there I couldn't stand it no longer. [*Sets down table.*] Fetch me a chair, Pompey. [*Exit* POMPEY L.] I'll finish my ironin' in here. [POMPEY *brings in chair, pair of muddy boots, blacking and brush.* MRS. HOUGH *arranges board on table and chair and* POMPEY *cleans boots.*] There, it ain't quite so bil-ir.' hot in here.

Pomp. Wh-e-e-e-w !

Mrs. H. Hard work, Pompey?

Pomp. Yes—don' see whar Mr. Halliday got all dis clay on dese boots. I'se gwine to sabe it an' start a brick-yard.

Mrs. H. What'd you do with all the bricks?

Pomp. Sell 'em ob course—any fool'd do dat. Wouldn't you?

Mrs. H. Of course *you* would, Pompey.

Pomp. Sartain—'spose I'd carry 'em 'round in my hat—say, ole woman?

Mrs. H. Old woman, indeed! What d'ye take me for, you black villain?

Pomp. Don' take ye fur nuffin—but de man wat took ye fur better or worser got de mos' ob de worser, I recken.

Mrs. H. Take that, you scoundrel.   [*Throws basket.*

Pomp. [*Dodging.*] Didn't I tole ye so? [*Resuming work.*] Dis am de mos' obstreperus mud I eber seed on a boot—it's a stiff-necked an' rebellyus peeple.

Mrs. H. When is Mr. Halliday goin', Pompey?

Pomp. On de fus train after dinnah. Dare, dem boots am done. Mos' broke my back ober 'em, too.   [*Rises.*

Mrs. H. When will he be back?

Pomp. To-morrer nite, on de las' train.   Ye see, he's bin speenid
as a witness in a lawsuit an' he's got to go.   [*Starts to go out* C. E.

Mrs. H. Where you goin'?

Pomp. Guess I'll hitch up de mule an' cart out my brick-yard.

Mrs. H. Never mind now.   Take this iron out and get me a hot
one. [*Exit* POMPEY L., *with flat-iron.*] It'll seem strange to have Mr.
Halliday stay away all night.   He hasn't done that afore in all the
ten years he's bin in this house.   I wonder who's goin' to stay with
Mr. Jeffreys to-night.

Enter POMPEY.

Pomp. [*Spitting on iron.*] Golly! how it sizzles.   Hot, ain't it?
[*Spits on it again and rubs it off with finger, burning himself.*] Oh-h-h-
oo-oo·ow!   [*Dropping iron and dancing around.*

Mrs. H. What on arth's the matter?

Pomp. [*Yelling.*] If you want any roas' niggah fur dinnah, jis
step rite up an' git a slice while it's hot.

Mrs. H. [*Picking up iron.*] Who's goin' to stay with Mr. Jeffreys
to-night?

Pomp. I is.   Gimme a rag.   [*She gives him one and he winds it on
finger.*

Mrs. H. You, Pompey?   Why, don't you know Mr. Jeffreys expects the Old Nick after him some night?

Pomp. No-o-o!   Gimme a rag.   [*Same business.*

Mrs H. 'Spose he'd come to-night.

Pomp. He won't come.

Mrs. H. What makes you think he won't come?

Pomp. 'Cause a 'spectable niggah like me don't keep cumpny wid
debbles, nohow.   Gimme a rag.

Mrs. H. Why, you black scoundrel, didn't I jest give you a rag?
Now shut your mouth an' help me carry out this table. [*Puts iron
on chair.   They carry table out* L, *and return.*] Now you take out the
flat-iron an' I'll take the board. [*Hands him iron.* POMPEY *spits on
it and she cuffs him.*] Take that, now.

Pomp. Oh-h-h!   Can't ye stop 'busin' a poor orfun?   Now I ain't
gwine to carry out dat iurn—it sizzles too much.   But you jis put
dat iurn rite back in dat char an' I'll carry de char out.

Mrs. H. All right.   [*She does so and exit* L. *with board.*

Pomp. [*Putting boots, blacking and brush into basket and coming
down front with chair.*] Dis niggah don' burn hissef on dat iurn agin.
[*Spits on it.*] No, sah!   it sizzles too much.   Yah, yah, yah!   Didn't
I make her bleeve I ain't 'fraid ob de debble?   But I ain't so shure
'bout dat.   Wish I was—but I ain't. [*Shaking head.*] Dat's wun ob
de unsartumties ob life.   But I'se in fur it now—an' lessee what I'll
do if he does come. [*Scratches head.*] Oh, yes!   I'll—[*Forgets himself
and sits down on iron, yells, jumps up and dances around.*] Oh-h, good
Lord! how dat sizzles.   It mus' a burned clar troo my bes' breeches
—to say nuffin at all 'bout how much furder. [*Picks up chair and
basket.*] Gimme a rag—gimme a hole sheet!   [*Exit* L.

SCENE IV.—JEFFREYS' *chamber ; bed* R.; *stand near it with lamp ; couch* L. *with pillow and blankets.* JEFFREYS *discovered in bed leaning on right elbow.*

Jeff. What is this strange feeling which so oppresses me to-night? Is it born of the weary past, the gloomy present or the awful future? Is it but a regret, springing from the many memories of my early love, which have recently been so vividly recalled? Is it but a loneliness, arising from the absence of my trusted companion—the first in all the years we have passed together? Or is it a foreshadowing of impending evil—a boding, which my anxious soul, restrained by its earthy tenement, can but vaguely comprehend? Can it be that the awful future is now—even NOW—pressing close upon me? Yet the thought of it does not terrify me, as once it did. No; I have been strangely calm since my interview with Nellie. I feel that my Helen, whom I so deeply wronged, has now forgiven me. I saw her in my dreams again, last night, and she no longer looked reproachfully upon me, but she smiled—she SMILED—and beckoned me to join her in that better land. Perhaps I may be permitted to do so. I feel a new-born hope—the first that has ever cheered my dreary lot—now strengthening within me. Perhaps the Lord has not utterly forsaken me. Pompey, bring me my Bible.

Enter POMPEY L., *with a large Bible.*

Pomp. Here it am, sah.   [*Acts nervous and excited.*
Jeff. Open it where the book-mark is and lay it on the stand. [*He does so and stands quietly by the bedside, while* JEFFREYS *reads aloud Psalm xxiii.*] Now, Pompey, you may lie down. It is late and I wish to be up betimes in the morning.   [*Lies down.*
Pomp. [*Aside.*] If he wants to git up so arly, why don' he sit up all nite? [*Looks all around, turns lamp low, lies down, jumps up and snuffs.*] Don' I smell brimstone smoke? [*Snuffs.*] Oh, no; it's wun ob dem cats wat carries a 'tumery bottle.

[POMPEY *lies down and covers head with blanket.—Stage dark.—A thunder storm comes up, gradually increasing in fury. The clock strikes twelve. A vivid flash of lightning is followed by a deafening crash of thunder. Enter* HOTALING, L., *disguised as devil, moving cautiously toward the bed.* POMPEY *awakes, peeps out from under blankets, then rolls off couch in terror, carrying pillow and blankets with him and rises up on knees.*

Pomp. Oh, good debble! I'se only a poor niggah—
Hot. Silence! [*Making a gesture toward* POMPEY, *who sinks on floor in abject terror, snatches up pillow, puts it on his head and holds it down to floor.* JEFFREYS *rises in bed and stares at* HOTALING *in horror.*] Samuel Jeffreys, I claim the forfeit.   [*Slowly approaching bed.*

Jeff. "My God, my God, why hast thou forsaken me?"

[JEFFREYS *sinks back with a groan.* HOTALING *springs upon the bed and grasps him by the throat.*

TABLEAU.

END OF ACT II.

ACT III.

SCENE I.—JEFFREYS' *office, as in Act I.* RICHARD *discovered seated near desk.*

Rich. The deed is done, the inquest held and the old man buried. I am now the sole owner of the accumulated wealth of the House of Jeffreys. Old Halliday was stricken down, as if by a thunder bolt, when he heard the news, and he is now a helpless imbecile. Hotaling must be many miles away from here, by this time. The impudent scoundrel found more money in the safe than I offered him, so he took that, escaped from the window and fled, carrying the will with him, instead of coming back to me. Lucky for him he did. How easy it would have been for me to send a bullet through his brain, silencing him forever. Then I could have told the startled household that I awoke, rushed from my room and met the villain in the hall, as he was escaping from my uncle's chamber. But that is one of my plans that didn't work. However, Hotaling is a prudent man and has a quiet tongue. Besides, he wrote me that he would destroy that will—so I may consider my plan a decided success. Now I will enjoy myself, for I have wealth enough and to spare.

[*A solemn voice is heard behind him. He starts up in fear. Enter* HALLIDAY, C. E., *wild and haggard in appearance, speaking as he comes down front.*

Hal. "Thou fool, this night thy soul shall be required of thee; then whose shall those things be, which thou hast provided?"

[RICHARD, *in a transport of rage, rushes at* HALLIDAY, *as if to strike him down.*

Rich. Back to your room, driveling idiot, ere I strike you to the earth!

Enter NELLIE C. E., *hurriedly.*

Nel. Father! where are you? [*Rushes between them.*] Stand back, Richard Jeffreys! No one but a coward would strike an old man.

Rich. Pardon me, Nellie, but his abrupt entrance and wild words startled me from a fit of deep meditation and I turned to meet the intruder, before I knew who it was. Strike your father? I hope you will not so misjudge me, Nellie.

Nel. I am very anxious about my father. I did not know that he had left his room until I came in just now and found him gone. I hope he will not trouble you again.

Rich. He'll be no trouble to me at all, Nellie. So let him come as often as he will into this room, where he has spent so many days with my uncle. I shall be happy to have him sit here in remembrance of his kindness to the poor old man. [*Aside.*] I'd rather see him in Tophet, though. [NELLIE *turns to go out with father.*] Let me assist you, Nellie.

Nel. No, thank you. I need no assistance. [*Exeunt* C. F.

Rich. I nearly spoiled my chances with Nellie that time. I have not said anything to her about my love, since the appearance of His Satanic Majesty—she has been so much engaged in caring for her father and I have had too much delicacy to intrude upon her sorrow. But I fancy that I have recommended myself as a candidate for her favors, by procuring the most skilful medical advice for her father and offering them both a home during his illness. I induced her to accept such favors by telling her I did it all in the name of my uncle. And then, I've reformed, too, and I am meditating the propriety of turning divinity student and plunging headlong into orthodox theology—all for Nellie. I'll have that girl yet—she's the one thing needful to complete my happiness. [*A gentle rap is heard* L.] Come in. [*Enter* MISS WYCKOFF.] Oh—ah—excuse me for not opening the door. I thought it was merely some gentleman on business.

Miss W. [*Haughtily.*] Make no apologies, sir. I have come on business and expect no better treatment than your other business callers receive.

Rich. Don't you? You're modest in your expectations. But be seated. [*They sit.*] What progress have you made?

Miss W. I have finished the letter. I have a large number of notes and letters, which Mr. Jennison has sent me, relative to my lawsuit and other business matters. So I have been able to pick out, one by one, all the peculiarities of his handwriting.

Rich. Well, now, Miss Wyckoff, you have a business way about you that I admire. What a magnificent forger you are!

Miss W. Sir! Mr. Jeffreys—

Rich. That's my name.

Miss W. Your impudence is past forbearance.

Rich. Yet you seem to bear it.

Miss W. [*Starting up.*] I will not any longer.

Rich. Yes, you will—you'll finish the business you came for.

Miss W. [*Spitefully.*] Not from any love for your company, however.   [*Resumes seat.*

Rich. But from an ardent desire to be revenged on Nellie Halliday, because her pretty face has won the admiration of Mr. Jennison. Now don't you think me a very successful mind-reader?

Miss W. I care nothing for your accomplishments in that direction.

Rich. Ah. indeed! Well, your desire for revenge overcomes your repugnance for me, and we work together for the same purpose. It's not the first time that two hostile forces have fought side by side against a common enemy.

Miss W. Since I am accommodating you quite as much as I am gratifying myself, you ought to be a little more civil, if you can be.

Rich. Well, I'll practice a little. Resume business.

Miss W. Mr. Jennison writes quite a light hand for a gentleman and I quite a heavy one for a lady. So I have been able to imitate his handwriting very successfully. Here is the letter. [*Handing it to him.*

Rich. [*Reading.*] "DEAR SIR:—In reference to the debt I owe you, I would say that I shall be amply able to pay it in full, after my marriage with Miss Wyckoff. Until then I ask your forbearance.   Yours &c.,

To RICHARD JEFFREYS, ESQ.   EDWARD JENNISON."

Miss Wyckoff, that is a masterly imitation of his handwriting. It would deceive Jennison himself.

Miss W. Show it to Nellie Halliday. If it deceives her, that is all I ask.

Rich. I will do so, but we run a great risk, If there is really an engagement between them, we may not succeed. [*Puts letter in desk.*

Miss W. I tell you there *is* no engagement—it is impossible—I don't believe it. Mr. Jennison is a man of too much sense to tie himself to a girl like her. Now they are both as proud as Lucifer, and if a doubt once comes between them—

Enter POMPEY L.

Rich. What now, Pompey?

Pomp. De masons am cum fur to fix dat seller wall you want mendid an' dey wants to see you. Dey's ready to go to work. [*Exit.*

Rich. Excuse me for a moment, Miss Wyckoff. I'll be back directly.   [*Exit L.*

Miss W. [*Rising.*] It cannot be that they are engaged—it *must* not be. I know that, if it were not for that Nellie Halliday, I could bring Mr. Jennison to a proposal at once. I have wealth enough for us both, and I want him for the position he can give me. He is a rising lawyer and is destined to make his mark in this world. My wealth will aid him greatly in his upward course—will open opportunities to him, which are almost, if not quite, denied to a poor man —such as he would be with Nellie Halliday, who has not a cent in the world.

NELLIE *raps* C. E. *and enters.*

Nel. Oh! excuse me, Miss Wyckoff. I thought Mr. Jeffreys was here

Miss W. He just stepped out. But come in, Miss Halliday. I wish to see you a moment. [NELLIE *comes down front.*] Do you love Edward Jennison?

Nel. [*Confused.*] I-I-I cannot answer that question.

Miss W. It is sufficiently answered by your manner. Will you give him up?

Nel. To you?

Miss W. Yes, to me.

Nel. Mr. Jennison will ask a release personally, when he desires one, and not through a second party.

Miss W. I can give him wealth and influence to assist him in winning that position in public life, which he is so well qualified to fill. But *you*—you would only be a dead weight to sink him deeper and deeper into obscurity. Think again, Miss Halliday — what can you offer such a man as Edward Jennison?

Nel. *I* can offer him a woman's love—an emotion to which your stony heart is a total stranger. *I* can offer him a woman's encouragement, and *that*, to him, will a prove a stronger incentive to work and win than all the wealth you could lavish upon him.

Miss W. Woman's fiddlesticks! Have you filled your mind with dish-water novels and sickish love stories, that you talk such nonsense to me?

Nel. He is too noble to purchase advancement in this world—least of all would he do it with the money of his wife.

Enter RICHARD L.

Rich. Ah! I see you have had pleasant company during my absence, Miss Wyckoff.

Miss W. Very pleasant, indeed. Miss Halliday is *so* entertaining.

Rich. [*Aside.*] I bet the fire flew when they struck. Two women after the same man wouldn't be very safe visitors in a powder-mill.

Miss W. I must bid you both good morning now.

Nel. Good morning.

Rich. [*Showing her out*] Good morning.   [*Exit* MISS W.

Nel. I must now return to my father. I only stepped in to tell you the masons had come, as I couldn't find Pompey to send to you.

Rich. I have just been out to see them. But wait a moment, Nellie. I wish to speak to you. Since my uncle's death I have refrained from speaking to you on that subject, which, you know, lies so near my heart. But I cannot postpone it any longer.

Nel. I cannot listen to you, Mr. Jeffreys.

Rich. My love for you is the same, Nellie, but I am a different man. My uncle's sad death and your own words have startled me into an awful realization of what my past life has been. It shall be such no longer.

Nel. I will be frank with you, Mr. Jeffreys. It is impossible for me to become your wife—I am already betrothed to Mr. Jennison.

Rich. [*Aside.*] Hell furies! Must I always have that man flung into my face? [*Aloud.*] Mr. Jennison, Nellie? That cannot be. He expects to marry Miss Wyckoff

Nel. Marry Miss Wyckoff!

Rich. That's what I said.

Nel. What do you mean, sir?

Rich. Just what I said.

Nel. Upon what do you base your opinion, pray?

Rich. Upon the very best foundation imaginable—he mentioned it to me in one of his business letters. I'll find it—it must be in my desk somewhere.   [*Looks for it.*

Nel. A letter from Edward Jennison, in which he tells *you* that he expects to marry Miss Wyckoff? Impossible, sir!

Rich. [*Aside.*] How it cuts her. I'll give her another thrust. [*Aloud.*] He is considerably in debt and expects to relieve himself from embarrassment as soon as he gets his hands on Miss Wyckoff's money.

Nel. Richard Jeffreys—

Rich He was considerably taken aback to learn that my uncle left you none of his property. So he has hit upon this new plan of relieving himself from financial difficulties. Ah! here's the letter. [*Handing it to her,*] You know his handwriting, I suppose.

Nel. Yes, I know it well—and this is his. [*Reads.*] Oh! what words are these!

Rich. [*Aside.*] I thought that letter would do it. [*Aloud.*] Now you see the difference between the mercenary passion of Edward Jennison and the sincere affection of Richard Jeffreys.

Nel. [*Excitedly.*] What! no date? Richard Jeffreys, this letter is a forgery!   [*Flings it down.*

Rich. [*Aside.*] Curse Miss Wyckoff's stupidity.

Nel. Edward Jennison never wrote that letter. No business man —much less a lawyer—would write so important a letter and omit the date.

Rich. I assure you, Nellie, it is no forgery of mine. I received that letter in the way of business.

Nel. [*Contemptuously.*] "Business!" Yes, if you call your contemptible plotting with Miss Wyckoff "business." I see it all now. I can understand why Miss Wyckoff wanted me to give up Mr. Jennison.

Rich. [*Aside.*] Damnation! was she such a fool as that?

Nel. Do not have the effrontery to tell me that he owes you a debt. He owed your uncle nothing. Before *his* death you had not a cent you could call your own—much less any indebtedness from Edward Jennison.

Rich. [*Aside.*] It's her turn to thrust now.

Nel. Nor is he so contemptible a creature as to marry any woman for her money and then take that money to pay his debts. You cannot comprehend true manhood, Richard Jeffreys, and you have mistaken your man. [*Exit.*

Rich. Wh-e-e-e-w! Disappeared in a thunder-gust! What a little vixen she is, really. I wouldn't take her for a wife, if I could have her just as well as not—and the prospects are that I shan't be troubled. How handsome she looked, though. And how she lashed me. Yet there was something refreshing about it. I'd rather be cuffed by such a woman than caressed by Miss Wyckoff. But isn't her faith in Jennison something sublime? It's a pity to spoil it—but I will. I'll find some blemish in his wonderful perfection. [*Picks up letter.*] Confound Miss Wyckoff for her stupid blunder. [*Tearing letter.*] If she had been blessed with one-tenth as much brains as Nellie has, we might have been successful. As it is, we are worse off than we were before. But we shall see. [*Exit* L.

SCENE II.—*Garden. Corner of* JEFFREYS' *house seen* L.

Enter NELLIE R.

Nel. How much longer must I remain in this house which has now become so hateful to me? Now that my poor father is able to be moved, his bewildered brain imagines this to be his daughter's house and he exclaims piteously against being driven from his Nellie's home. Yet I cannot remain here longer as a dependant upon Richard's bounty. What shall I do? I have no one to advise me now, but Edward. And shall I go to him? Yes, yes, I will. I know he never wrote that letter. [*Approaching house.*] 'Twas from this window that the murderer escaped, after the commission of his horrid crime. Oh! was it not cruel enough to murder the kind old man, without taking advantage of his strange delusion and making death doubly terrible to him? Methinks I see him now, yielding to his fate, in the firm conviction that the Lord had forsaken him and had allowed the Evil One to drag his soul down, down into perdition. [*Starts.*] Ha! what's that—half buried in the sand? [*Picks up knife.*] A knife! and marked with the letter "H." God grant that this may prove a clue to the detection of the murderer. [*Exit.*

Enter POMPEY R., *carrying in one hand a watering-pot, with the spout broken off, and holding a rooster by the legs, in the other hand.*

Pomp. Oh, deah! wish I'd bin born in two volumes—like de Skiamese twins. Den I mite a done two tings to wunst an' bin a happy niggah. But I only cum wun at a time an' de udder fellah aint got along yit, so I'm de mos' misable niggah on dis yerth. It's hard enuff, de Lord knows, fur me to do wun ting to a time—'speshally if I don' feel disposed—but when de folks tole me to do two tings to wunst, I 'sider it's imposin' on dis niggah's good nature. Now dare's Miss Nellie, she tole me fur to take de waterin' pot an' sprinkle water all ober her sun-flowers, an' unyuns, an' dandeliums, an' beets

an' hollyhocks, an' cabbiges—an' den Mrs. Hough, she tole me fur
to cotch de ole red rooster an' kill him fur dinnah. Den I got so
mixed up dat I'll be doggoned if didn't run down de waterin' pot
an' sprinkle de ole rooster all ober de posy bed. Golly! didn't he
squawk. Well, de fact ob de hole business is, I aint had no cumfurt since ole Mr. Jeffreys died. De fust ting wat happened to worry me was dat corner's inquest—thought dey nebber would git troo
wid it. It took three lawyers, six jurymen an' an ole bull head ob
a Justis ob de Peeses a hole day to find out if de ole man was ded.
Dat's wat cums ob studyin' law so much—it always makes a man
slow to know anyting. Now I knowed it all de time—an' dat's de
fus time I knowed wun niggah's hed am worf more'n ten white
wuns. An den de lawyers tried to make me bleeve it wasn't de
debble dat choked Mr. Jeffreys. Wasn't I dare? Didn't I see him
—an' smell him? Who in de debble was it, if it wasn't de debble?
An' dat's de way it goes—trials, troubles an' tribulations fur dis
niggah all de time. De only way I has to cheer me is to warble
some little upper-attic air—like dis wun:

[*Singing.*]   De rooster am a purty bird,
          He libs on wums an' corn;
      He wakes us in de mornin' up
          A blowin' on his horn.

      His legs am like two crooked sticks,
          His nose am built ob horn;
      He hasn't got no teef at all
          To chaw de Ingin corn,

      He flies on top de chickin coop
          De country fur to view;
      Den flops his wings an' sings his song—
          His cock-a-doodle-doo.

      He flies into de garden beds,
          An' scratches wid his toes;
      An' when he finds an angle-wum
          He eats him wid his nose.

      But dis one here no more will eat
          De angle-wums an' corn;
      No more he'll wake dis niggah up
          Wid his bugle in de morn.

Mrs. H. [*Outside* L.] Pompey-y-y.
Pomp. (*Imitating tone of voice.*) What-y-y-y?
Mrs. H. Caught that rooster yet?
Pomp. Yes-s-s-s.
Mrs. H. Chopped his head off yet?
Pomp. Yes-s-s-s.

Enter Mrs. Hough.

Mrs. H. There! you've bin lyin' to me.   Don't I see his head on him yet?

Pomp. [*Looking first at rooster and then at watering-pot.*] Gosh! dat cums ob tryin' to do two tings to wunst.   I'll be doggoned if I didn't chop de snout off de ole waterin' pot.

Mrs. H. Go rite back an' chop his head off.   [*Exit* L.

Pomp. Dare's nuffin like trouble to make a niggah's head swim.
                                                        [*Exit* R.

———

SCENE III.—Jennison's *law office.*   Jennison *discovered seated at desk* R. H.

Jen. The jury rendered a verdict of death "at the hands of some person unknown, which person was disguised as Satan."   What else could they do?   They had only the testimony of Pompey, as to what transpired in the chamber on that fatal night, and he—poor simple fellow—couldn't tell his story twice alike.   No one else knew anything about the matter.   Whoever is guilty of the murder, laid his plans shrewdly and has most successfully covered up his tracks. [*Rising and pacing slowly back and forth.*] He was no stranger—that's certain, and I more than half believe that Richard could tell more than he will.   A lawyer should be the last man to suspect another of crime without any evidence, but I cannot help feeling that he was in some way concerned in his uncle's "taking off."   At any rate, I will keep a close watch upon him.

Enter Miss Wyckoff L.

Miss W. Good afternoon, Mr. Jennison.

Jen. Good afternoon.   Be seated, please.   [*They sit.*

Miss W. I just dropped in, as I was passing, to see how my case is getting along.

Jen. I have received a letter from Messrs Quirk & Quibble, attorneys for defendant, stating that they are willing to settle.

Miss W. Indeed!   Well, I thought your shrewdness and ability would soon bring them to terms.

Jen. [*Aside.*] Now for some soft soap.

Miss W. I cannot expect to profit by the services of so able a lawyer without paying well for them. [*Opening purse.*] Here are $50 more for your services.

Jen. Not now, Miss Wyckoff, thank you.   Wait until the case is finally disposed of.

Miss W. Just as you wish, Mr. Jennison, but I shall insist upon paying you well. [*Rising.*] Good afternoon.   [*Exit* L.

Jen. That woman fondly thinks her case one of the most difficult that ever graced the calendar of the Circuit Court, when in fact it is as clear as the sunlight which streams through my office window. But that is a common delusion on the part of clients. It is seldom, however, that a lawyer tires of receiving pay, but if I am heartily sick and tired of anything in this world, it is that woman's purse—and soft soap. I really believe she would give me her whole fortune—her own precious self included—if I should give her half a chance.

Enter NELLIE L.

Nel. Good afternoon, Edward.

Jen. Why, good afternoon, Nellie. This is an agreeable surprise.

Nel. May I ask you a question, Edward?

Jen. Certainly you may—a dozen, if you wish. But be seated first, [*They sit.*] It isn't very often that I have a young lady for a client and I rather enjoy it.

Nel. But you often have a *rich* one.

Jen. Yes—I just had a severe attack of that complaint. The attacks are very regular. But you are forgetting your question.

Nel. Do not think me impudent, Edward, but—but—

Jen. But what, Nellie?

Nel. Do you owe Richard Jeffreys anything?

Jen. Not a cent. Why do you ask?

Nel. I will explain at another time. I have more important business now.   [*Takes out knife.*

Jen. Well, if that's the way all young lady clients come prepared, I'll steer clear of them. I hope you didn't come here with any malice aforethought.

Nel. None whatever—unless it be toward the man who lost this knife.

Jen. I do not understand you, Nellie.

Nel. I found this knife, this morning, beneath the window from which the murderer escaped. I hope it may prove a clue to the mystery.   [*Hands it to him.*

Jen. I hope it may. I see its handle is marked with the letter "H." May I keep it, Nellie?

Nel. Certainly.

Jen. In all the history of crime, I can recall no murder that was more skilfully planned than this. I have studied the case carefully and I trust that this knife will aid me in my further investigations.

Nel. Have you any theory in regard to the murder?

Jen. Who was most benefited by the death of Mr. Jeffreys?

Nel. Why—Richard, I suppose—but—

Jen. Exactly, keep that point in view. Now, the crime must have been committed by some one who was—

(1) Familiar with Mr. Jeffreys' rooms;

(2) Acquainted with his strange delusion;

(3) Cognizant of the fact that your father would be away that night.

Richard had incurred many gambling debts and was sorely pressed for money. He was his uncle's only heir. He has a wicked, malicious disposition. On the morning before the murder, I met him in the street, and when I declined to yield to him as a suitor for your hand, he told me he had a faculty of clearing his pathway before him. When he forebade my entering his uncle's house again and I told him he had no right to do so, he remarked that he might have a right sooner than I expected. Add to all this, his indifference, his refusal to contribute toward the reward offered and his determined opposition to the employment of an experienced detective—

Nel. [*All excitement.*] Denounce the villain to the world!

Jen. Not yet, Nellie. These things are hardly legal proofs.

Nel. You lawyers are always so slow!

Jen. But sure, Nellie. Richard is shrewd—fertile in resources. He has wealth and influence and we must not even let him know that he is suspected, until we have a clear case. Then we can crush him at once with the full force of it. There is such a thing, too, as our being mistaken. I do not think it was Richard's hand, however, that strangled his uncle. He probably had an accomplice, and that accomplice is, doubtless, the owner of this knife.

Nel. But what shall I do? I cannot remain in that house any longer—yet my poor father objects to our leaving.

Jen. Why so?

Nel. He imagines that it is his Nellie's house and he says he will not be driven from her home.

Jen. What makes him think it is your house?

Nel. I cannot tell, unless it is because we have lived there so long.

Jen. Does he talk of anything else?

Nel. I have heard him talk in a rambling way about a will.

Jen. Indeed! We may discover something more than a murderer, Nellie.

Nel. Discover *him* and I shall be satisfied. [*Rises.*

Jen. [*Rising.*] While you are reconciling your father to a removal, you may discover more. Come to me again on Thursday. Meanwhile I will be on the alert.

Nel. I will do so. Good afternoon.

Jen. Good afternoon. [*Showing her out.*] The first clue, although it does not point directly to Richard. I will see that this knife is carefully secured. [*Puts it in pocket.*] And now for my afternoon's mail. [*Exit L.*

SCENE IV.—*Woods.*

Enter PYMAKER R., *tramping back, having a new tail on his coat, of a different color from the rest of it.*

Py. [*Tripping and falling headlong.*] "Slap, bang, here we are again!" [*Getting up.*] That twig rather upset my dignity—or what

there is left of it, for I confess it's badly decayed. I think I may
safely return to the village now. I've been engaged in the *retailing*
business since I left here, [*Showing coat-tail.*] and the marshal won't
know me now. My conscience has troubled me continually since
that evening in the woods. I ought to have returned at once to
thwart the plans of those two villains, if possible. But I'll return
now and do what I can to ferret them out. But first let me practice
my new song a little more, before I present it to an appreciative
audience.   [*Clears throat during prelude and sings:*

> Through the forest shades I tramp, thinking, mother dear, of you.
> And the good and wholesome fare I once enjoyed;
> And the tears they fill my eyes, spite of all that I can do,
> For my stomach seems a vast and boundless void.

> Tramp, tramp, tramp, I'm sadly marching,
> Look out, housewives, I advance;
> And beneath my ragged vest there's an "aching void" to fill
> With your meat, potatoes—cake and pie, perchance.
> [*A bell is heard in the distance.*

Hark! I hear the village bells ringing for noon. I shall be late
to dinner.   [*Exit* L.

———

SCENE V.—O'BLARNEY'S *groggery; an old bar* L. H.; *table and chairs*
R. H.; 1 L. E. *leading to street;* U. L. E. *to kitchen;* 1 R. E. *to sit-*
ting-room; U. R. E. *to* HOTALING'S *room.* O'BLARNEY *discovered*
behind counter drinking.

Mich. Och! but whishky's a moighty foine thing in the roight
place. [*Leaning on counter.*] Now, be the Howly Vargin, but it's
moighty hard for an honesht boy loike me to arn a daycint livin'.
A few wakes ago I sold my ould mither's lasht cow an' bot a shmall
shtock o' whishky an' shtarted this jewil uv a bordin' house. The
ould lady objicted at firsht, but whin I tould her ye moight as well
thry to raise praties in yer hat as to run a daycint bordin' house
widout whishky, she saw the force o' me argymint at once. [*Mixes*
another drink.] It was milk ur whishky wid us thin, so we thot we'd
shquaze along widout the milk an'—[*Drinks.*] Och! but whishky's
a moighty foine thing in the roight place. But now me shtock o'
whishky's almosht gone. An' me ould nither kapes a tazin' an' a
tazin' for the pay for the cow, an' it's little pace o' moind she gives me
whiniver she's around, till I gives her a dhrop o' whishky, an' that
makes her furgit her ould cow. It makes her talk, too, but that's a
wakeness uv her sex.   [*Drinks,*

Enter MRS. O'BLARNEY 1 R. E.

Mrs. O'B. The top o' the mornin' till yez, Michel
Mich. An' the bottom o' me tumbler. [*Aside.*] Now for the ould
cow again.

Mrs. O'B. Dhrinkin' agin', Michel, an' not offrin' your poor ould mither a dhrop!—an' she a nadin' the pay for her cow.

Mich. Tazin' agin, mither! Why can't ye hould yer ould tung an' let a poor boy alone, till he can arn the money to pay yez?

Mrs. O'B. Och! Michel, it's toime I've bin a givin' yez for foive long wakes, an' not a blissid cint have I got for me waitin' ayther. An' it's a wishin' that I am that I had me ould cow back agin. (*Sobbing.*) She was the thwatest baste that iver shtraddled a pail. She niver shwitched her tail intil me face in all the tin long years I had her. (*Sobs violently.*) It makes the tears come intil my ould eyes ivery toime I think uv her—

Mich. Oh, shtop yer blarney, mither!

Mrs. O'B. Och! Michel, it's little Bridget O'Toole thot, whin she marrid Barney O'Blarney, that her ildest son would iver teil his poor widdid mither to shtop her blarney—an' she a' nadin' the pay for her cow—in' him wid a hole dhrawer full o' money the hole blissid toime.

Mich. Divil a cint hiv I got in the dhrawer. (*Showing it.*) See that now. But come, mither, let me fix yez up sumthin hot an' shtrong, afore ye go out into the shtrate this mornin'.

Mrs. O'B. (*With signs of satisfaction.*) Arrah, me honey! it's many a talk that I've had with yer poor ded father, a tellin' him that it was Michel, that'd be a cumfurt an' a blessin' to his poor mither in her ould age. But only a dhrop, Michel—on.y a dhrop.
(*Leans over bar.*

Mich. (*Handing her liquor.*) Och! mither, but whishky's a moighty foine thing in the roight place. Ye loike it yersilf better'n milk.

Mrs. O'B. Ach-b-h! Michel, don't talk to me uv milk, whin I've a dhrop uv this afore me. Milk turns me shtomach loike wather.

Enter HOTALING, U. R. E., *limping.*

Mich. An' ye concluded to git up, did ye? It's a long whoile pas thrain toime ye've bin shlapin', Mr. Hotaling. Ye won't be afther lavin' us to-day, will ye?

Hot. (*Sitting down by table.*) Why in h—l didn't you wake me up in time for the train, you fool?

Mich. Indade, Mr. Hotaling, an' I shtuck me hed intil yer room a short toime ago, an' yer nose was singin' sich a shwate lullaby intil yer ears, that I hadn't the hart to waken yez at all, at all.

Mrs. O'B. I guess I'll be afther makin' Mr. Hotaling's bed now.
(*Exit* U. R. E.

Hot. Well, I must stay here till night now, so fix me up something hot and strong, Michel.

Mich. All roight—I'll go an' git sum hot wather. (*Exit* U. L. E., *with pitcher.*

Hot. (*Putting hands to head.*) Will this cursed pain never cease? My head will burst! All night long this steady throbbing of my temples has tortured me, as if some fiend, with measured blows, were driving a wedge into my head, to cleave my skull, dash out my brains and disclose my secret thoughts unto the world. And the old man's cry is ringing in my ears. Never, until they are deaf in death, will they cease to hear that cry. I must fly from this accursed place. Had I not sprained my ankle, when I leaped from the old man's window, I would have been far away from here, ere this.

[HOTALING *bows head on table. Enter a* BOY, *who posts up a notice of* $300 *Reward for the arrest of the thief who stole* MISS WYCKOFF'S *silver, marked "*J. G. W." *and exit* 1 L. E.

Enter MICHEL *with pitcher.*

Mich. I'll soon have it ready for yez an' it'll do yez good.
Hot. Hurry up.
Mich. I'm a comin', Mr. Hotaling. (*Taking it to him.*) Here it is shtamin' hot an' shtrong as Samson.

[MICHEL *sets the liquor on table and then goes up and reads notice of Reward, pointing as if spelling out each word.* HOTALING *sips liquor and then absent-mindedly takes spoon from pocket and stirs his drink.*

Hot. [*Aside.*] Curse the luck! I don't like to hang around here another day.
Mich. [*To himself.*] Three hundred dollars reward for the man that shtole Miss Wyckoff's silver, marked "J. G. W." Bedad! if I could only git the reward, the poor divel that did the shtalin' moight go. [*Turns and sees* HOTALING.] A shpoon! I niver seen him have that afore. [*Creeps up cautiously and looks over his shoulder.*
Hot. [*Aside.*] Jeffreys thinks me many miles away from here by this time. I've got the will yet and a d—d sight more money than he offered me.
Mich. [*Aside.*] Fwat a purty shpoon! Solid silver, too! Fwat's that he's a talkin' about now?   [*Listens.*
Hot. [*Aside*] $2,000 reward for the criminal, eh?
Mich. [*Aside.*] No, bedad! it's only $300. Howly Mowses! fwat's thim letters on that shpoon?—"J. G. W."—an' "W" shtands for "Wyckoff." I'll hav him arreshted an' git the reward. [*Goes to bar.*

Enter PYMAKER 1 L. E.

Py. How are you, O'Blarney?
Mich. Foine, Mr. Pymaker, an' how's yersilf?
Py. As well as could be expected of a man that slept in a dry goods box.
Mich. An' didn't ye hav nuthin at all to kape yez warm?
Py. Not a drop.
Mich. [*Leading him down front.*] Now, if ye'll tind me bar jist two minnits, whoile I shtep out, ye may hav all ye wants.
Py. Agreed!   [*Goes behind bar.*
Mich. [*Aside.*] I'll go an' foind an officer.   (*Exit* 1 L. E.

Py. All I want, eh ? That's what I call a "phat take." I'll proceed to take it.   (*Drinks and fills bottle.*

Hot. (*Aside.*) I wonder where I lost that knife. If I dropped it in the old man's chamber, it's all up with me, unless I get away from here, and that pretty soon. (*Drinks liquor and puts spoon into pocket.*

Enter MICHEL, 1 L. E., *with an* OFFICER.

Mich. (*Pointing.*) That's him—that's him.
Py. (*Aside*) My clerkship's o'er.   *Exit* 1 L. E. *with bottle.*

[HOTALING *rises and starts for his room.* OFFICER *stops him.* O'-BLARNEY *misses one bottle and chases* PYMAKER *to the door.*

Off. Stop! you are my prisoner.   (*Laying hand on shoulder.*
Hot. (*Staggering back.*) For what ?
Off. For robbing Miss Wyckoff's house on the night of the 10th.
Hot. (*Recovering composure.*) Why am I charged with that ?
Off. You have part of the stolen property on your person now a silver spoon marked "J. G. W."
Hot. If this is what you mean, you are welcome to it. (*Handing spoon.*) I can easily account for my possession of that spoon. So take me off. (*Aside.*) Curse it! I must put on a bold face, but I fear this will get me into still deeper trouble.   (*Exeunt* 1 L. E.
Mich. Wh-oo-oo-p! yip! (*Tossing up hat.*) I'll git me reward, pay me ould mither fur her cow an' lay in a shtock o' whishky. An' now I'll take a dhrop to cilebrate me good luck. (*Drinks.*) Och! but whishky's—

Enter MRS. O'BLARNEY, U. R. E., *screaming.*

Mrs. O'B. Oh-h-h-oo-oo! Michel, Michel, sind fur the praste sind fur the praste!   [*Falls on floor.*
Mich. [*Helping her into a chair.*] Fwat in the divil's the matter wid yez, mither ?
Mrs. O'B. Oh! Michel, I was jist a workin' in Mr. Hotaling's room—a shwapin' an' a dustin' by the big chimney over the ould foire-place—whin down fell the divil's hole shkin—harns, tail an' all—roight down be me fate. Oh, Michel, sind fur the praste!
Mich. Yer an ould fool, mither. Fwat d've shpose the divil'd lave his shkin in the ould chimney fur? I'll go an' see mesilf fwat it is that shcared yez.   [*Exit.*
Mrs. O'B. Oh, wurra, wurra, wurra, wurra, wurra. Little did Bridget O'Toole think, whin she marrid Barney O'Blarney, that the divil would iver cum intil her house to shkin himsilf—the dhirty baste that he is.

Enter MICHEL, *with hair erect, dragging the disguise after him in the tongs.*

Mich. It's the divil's own shkin, mither. He must a cum afther Mr. Hotaling fur shtalin' Miss Wyckoff's silver an' got cot in the chimney an' left his shkin behoind him.   [*Holding it up.*

Mrs. O'B. Sind fur the praste, Michel—sind fur Father McTilligan !

TABLEAU.

END OF ACT III.

ACT IV.

SCENE I.—*Jail.* HOTALING R. H. *and* PYMAKER L. H. *discovered as prisoners.*

Py. Here I am, "locked up" and ready to "go to press," and I expect the "press gang" after me any minute. Egad ! but I had a glorious, rip-roaring old jamboree, before the marshal nabbed me. Drank more liquor than I've had before in six months, thanks to O'Blarney's generosity. And now I must be dealt with "according to the statutes in such case made and provided." I haven't a cent to pay a fine with, so I am fearful that I may have to languish in "durance vile" for some time to come. Then how can I ferret out those two villains? "Ay, there's the rub there's the respect that makes calamity of so long" an imprisonment. But there's the gentleman that occupied the cell next to mine last night. I'll address him. How are you, neighbor?

Hot. So-so, I believe you're the latest arrival. How do you like your quarters?

Py. Would like 'em better, if I could leave 'em sooner. [*Aside.*] I've heard that voice before.

Hot. What you here for?

Py. "Drunk and disorderly," I believe they term it.

Hot. You'll get out soon, I suppose.

Py. Would if I had the wherewithal to discharge my fine. [*Aside.*] Where have I heard that voice before?

Hot. Perhaps I can help you.

Py. Can you? Well, I'm an eligible subject for a little brotherly kindness—I am, indeed.

Hot. If you will do me a favor as soon as you are out, I'll furnish you the money to pay your fine.

Py. [*Aside.*] That voice! that form! by Jove, I'm on the scent!

Hot. You hesitate.

Py. Oh, no! I was only thinking. What can I do for you?

Hot. I want you to carry a note to a friend of mine.

Py. It's a bargain.

Hot. [*Writing on leaf of diary.*] I was arrested yesterday, in O'Blarney's saloon, for burglary, because I happened to have in my possession a silver spoon, marked "J. G. W."

Py. [*Aside.*] "J. G. W." eh? I see daylight ahead! It's Villain No. 1.

Hot. Although I am innocent of the crime charged against me, very likely I shall have to stay here for some time

Py. Yes; stolen property found on one's person is a very bad thing. [*Aside.*] Glad I lost that spoon.

Hot. I know it is—but I found the spoon in the woods one evening, where I supposed it had been lost by some picnic party.

Py. [*Aside.*] A picnic party consisting of ONE—and an old soup bone.

Hot. Although that is the fact, it may trouble me some to prove it.

Py. [*Aside.*] Wonder if I couldn't help him. Guess I won't, though. (*Aloud.*) Yes, that might trouble you some, if you were alone at the time.

Hot. No one was near.

Py. (*Aside.*) That's all he knows about it—don't think I'll enlighten him just now.

Hot. (*Tearing out leaf.*) Now I've written a note and I want it taken to Mr. Richard Jeffreys and no one else.

Py. (*Aside.*) Jeffreys! That's where the murder was committed —$2,000 reward—perhaps I'll see Villain No. 2.

Hot. Why do you hesitate so?

Py. I'm not hesitating—only thinking how to do it. But what shall I call you? We've never had the pleasure of an introduction.

Hot. Hotaling—Jack Hotaling. Your name?

Py. Pymaker—Benjamin Franklin Pymaker—a devotee of the "art preservative of all arts."

Hot. And a good judge of prime whiskey.

Py. Which the same is more to the point, I admit.

Hot. Well, here's the note. (*Giving it to him.*) Now how much money will you need to pay your fine?

Py. [*Aside, counting on fingers.*] Now there's $5 for fine, $2 for board and $1 for incidentals—$8. [*Aloud.*] Well, I guess you'd better let me have $30.

Hot. Here's the money. Now I shall depend upon you to deliver that note.

Py. It shall be delivered, sir, just as soon as old Justice Puffball pronounces me a free man once more.

Enter OFFICER L.

Off. Pymaker, this way.

Py. Hello! there's the "press gang." [*Striking an attitude.*] Would you drag me before the "minions of the law?"

Off. Don't worry—you'll be back soon enough.

Py. Now don't be too sure of that. But say, old Handcuffs, I owe you an everlasting debt of gratitude for locking me up here.

Off. An everlasting debt?

Py. Well—yes—did you ever know me to owe a debt that wasn't everlasting? But I've had a fine time in here—met an old friend—

Off. Come now—no more words.   [*Exeunt* L.

Hot. If I can only let Jeffreys know where the will and the disguise are, before they are discovered, I may keep myself out of deeper trouble, while I work out of this. But I am afraid they'll search my room for the stolen silver and find them both. But I'll go back to my cell and lie down—I don't feel well this morning. Although it seems an age to me, 'twas but one brief week ago tonight that I—Oh, God! I cannot speak it.   [*Exit* R.

— ——

SCENE II.—*Street.*

Enter PYMAKER L.

Py. There, that spree is paid for, and now for business. I know it's violating a sacred confidence reposed in me to read this note, but I'm a detective now and not a letter carrier. So here goes. (*Reading.*) "JEFFREYS:—You'll find that doc in my room—at O'Blarney's—beneath loose board in floor—under bed—and the masquerade in the chimney—secure them at once—I'm in limbo—JACK." D-o-c, doc. Now what does that mean? D-o-c, doc. Doctor? Have they been murdering some poor pill-peddler for his saddle-bags, and hid the corpus under the floor? Doc—doc—opodeldoc—burdock—dry-dock—Modoc—doxology—oh! perhaps he means "pub. doc." And then there's the "masquerade in the chimney." Rather close quarters for a successful masquerade, unless given by the chimney swallows. I know what he means by "in limbo"—been there myself. That's the only intelligible sentence in the whole note—that's classic English. "Doc—masquerade in the chimney." I give it up. This detective business is rather too much for me and I'm getting badly muddled. Hello! there's Mrs. O'Blarney coming. I'll buy an apple of her to make her good-natured and then see what I can get out of her.

Enter MRS. O'BLARNEY, R. H., *with a basket of apples.*

Mrs. O'B. Good mornin', Mr. Pymaker.

Py. Why, how do you do, Mrs. O'Blarney—you're looking remarkably fine to-day.

Mrs. O'B. Faith an' that's jist wat Michel was a tellin' me whin I shtarted out this mornin.' He tould me I looked as fresh an' bloomin' as the sunflowers in the back gardin. But it's the clothe-that does it, Mr. Pymaker—me new gown an' bunnit.

Py. Well, how do you sell apples?

Mrs. O'B. Pinny apace—fur as noice an apple as iver ye saw.

Py. Now that's too much. You ought to sell one and a hall for a cent.

Mrs. O'B. That's purty chape now, Mr. Pymaker, but, seein' yer one o' Michel's ould frinds an' cushtomers, I'll do it.

Py. All right—give me a cent's worth.   [*Offering cent.*

Mrs. O'B. Ah-h, ye shpalpane, d'ye think I'm a goin' to shplit one o' thim purty apples? By two cints' worth.

Py. That's more than I want. Let me have the two whole ones and trust me for the hall.

Mrs. O'B. Thrusht yez? Indade an' I won't. The divil only knows whin ye'd have any money agin. How'd ye cum to have so much by yez this mornin'?

Py. Struck a big bonanza. Here's your two cents.

Mrs. O'B. An' here's yer apples.

Py. (*Confidentially.*) Say, Mrs. O'Blarney, did you ever have a boarder by the name of Hotaling?

Mrs. O'B. Indade we did, an' Michel had him arreshted fur shtalin' Miss Wyckoff's shpoons. An' fwat d'ye shpose we found in the big chimney over the ould foire-place in his room?

Py. Can't tell. What was it?

Mrs. O'B. The ould divil's shkin—horns, tail an' all.

Py. (*Aside.*) By Jove! that's the "masquerade in the chimney." (*Aloud.*) Did you find anything else?

Mrs. O'B. An' wasn't that enuff? It sheared me out o' me foive sinses.

Py. Where's the skin now?

Mrs. O'B. Michel's got it.

Py. Tell him to keep it till I come—I want to see it. Good morning.   [*Exit* R. *hurriedly.*

Mrs. O'B. Faith, an' he goes off loike a shky-rocket. Well, I'll go home an' see wat Michel's a doin'. It's but a poor thrade I've bin a dhrivin' this mornin'. Havn't sould enuff to by the salt fur me petaties.   [*Exit* L.

SCENE III.—JENNISON'S *law office.* JENNISON *discovered sitting at* desk R. H.

Jen. No further developments relative to the murder. The only suspicious character hereabouts, whose name begins with "H," is Jack Hotaling. As the burglary took place on the same night as the murder, it is scarcely probable that he was concerned in both. However, I'll inquire of O'Blarney whether he has ever seen him have such a knife as this.

Enter POMPEY L.

Pomp. Good mornin', Mr. Jennison. Miss Nellie sent me heah fur to tole you she am a comin' in a few minnits fur to see you.

Jen. Very well—sit down, Pompey.

Pomp. Now I'se heah, Mister Jennison, I wants to **ax** your 'pinyun 'bout a wery important question ob law, dat's a gwine to disturb de frendly relations at present existin' between me an' my brudder Cicero. You know my brudder?

Jen. No, Pompey, but I should be happy to form his acquaintance.

Pomp. [*Jumping up.*] Would you? I'll go an' fotch him.

Jen. Not now—go on with your case.

Pomp. [*Sitting down.*] Well, ye see, I lent my brudder $10 las' fall, fur to help him by a cow. We made a sollum 'greement dat I was to have de fust caff wat dat cow had, fur de intres' on my munny You understand?

Jen. Perfectly.

Pomp. Well, what d'ye spose dat ole cow did las' spring?

Jen. Had a calf like a sensible cow.

Pomp Dat ole fool cow up an' had two caffs, an' de question am, Which am de fust caff? We's bin 'sputin' ober it eber sense.

Jen. [*Laughing.*] Why, Pompey, that's a question for the jury to determine.

Pomp. Well, how'll de jury know nuffin 'bout. it 'less dey have a lawyer fur to tole 'em?

Jen. I'll think of your case. And now, Pompey, I want to ask you a question. What did you see the night Mr. Jeffreys was murdered?

Pomp. Oh, can't ye give a poor niggah a rest on dat subject?

Jen. No rest until I learn all about it.

Pomp. [*Looking nervously around.*] I-I-I don' like to talk 'bout it heah.

Jen. What are you afraid of?

Pomp. My ole granfadder tole me dat de debble hangs round a lawyer's office mos' ob de time.

Jen. Your old grandfather never studdied law and didn't know much about it.

Pomp. No—he studdid gospel, an' dat's why he knows *all* 'bout it.

Jen. Well, he never comes in the daytime—so tell me what you saw.

Pomp. [*Hesitatingly.*] De debble, shuah. .

Jen. What else?

Pomp. His horns, an' hoofs, an' tail.

Jen. Is that all?

Pomp. His tail wound round him sebenteen times an' had a big speer hed on it.

Jen. Tell me the whole story, Pompey.

Pomp. De hole room was full o' brimstone smoke, an' it choked dis niggah mos' to def, an' I swoonded, an' den de debble nocked me down wid de pillah, an' tole me to shut my mouf, an' den he cum an' sot down on de pillah, an' put it on dis niggah's head, an' jammed my face rite down on de floah an' sot dare while he choked Mr. Jeffreys, an' dat's all I know 'bout it.

Enter NELLIE L.

Nel. Good morning, Edward.

Jen. [*Rising.*] Good morning, Nellie.

Pomp. You don't cotch dis niggah in a lawyer's office agin. [*Exit.*

Nel. Have you learned anything further yet?

Jen. I have not—but be seated.

Nel. Not now, I cannot stay long. I have determined to leave Mr. Jeffreys' house. Father has finally consented.

Jen. When do you leave?

Nel. To-morrow. I have remained there a week since Mr. Jeffreys died, and I can endure it no longer.

Jen. It is probably best—but where are you going?

Nel. Anywhere to get out of that house.

Jen. [*Taking her hand.*] I wish you would let me provide you both with a home. Before Mr. Jeffreys' death you told me to wait, because you could not leave him then. Now he is gone and you have no home. What is there to prevent our marriage now, Nellie?

Nel. Much as I love you, Edward, I could not consent to become your wife now and burden you with the care of my poor father.

Jen. But *you* cannot take care of him. Strive as hard as you may, you cannot provide him such care as he needs.

Nel. I will work night and day for him and deny myself everything, before he shall want such care.

Jen. But you are a woman, Nellie, and you must expect no more than a woman's remuneration for your work. That will not enable you to care for him as well as my income would, even though my practice is yet small.

Nel. Do not urge me now. We have a little means to rely upon for the present, and there is still something coming to father from Mr. Jeffreys' estate. So we are not entirely destitute.

Jen. I will not urge you now, as I am confident that the future has brighter days in store for you both.

Nel. It looks a little dark now, but I am not discouraged. I must go now. Good morning.

Jen. Good morning. [*Exit* NELLIE L.] God bless her! She is a brave girl, but she will have her courage sorely tried in caring for her poor stricken father. His needs will be many and her resources will be few. It is, indeed, a strange thing if Mr. Jeffreys—much as he thought of her father—did not make any provision for him, in any way. I cannot believe that he would be so thoughtless, when he expected to be taken away at any moment.

Enter MISS WYCKOFF L.

Miss W. Good morning, Mr. Jennison. I thought I would just run in and see how my case is progressing.

Jen. [*Aside.*] Confound her case.

Miss W. Have you any further information to give me?

Jen. Nothing further.

Enter PYMAKER L.

Py. Oh—ah—Miss Wyckoff, I believe.   [*Bowing low.*

Miss W. [*Haughtily.*] Why do you speak to me, sir?

Py. I believe we have met before.   [*Another low bow.*

Miss W. Yes—I recognize you as the tramp that stole one of my spoons the other day.

Py. [*Bowing.*] I had the honor, I believe.

Miss W. And I more than half believe you are the thief that stole my silver last week.

Py. [*Bowing.*] I had *not* the honor, Miss Wyckoff.

Jen. Have you any business with me, sir?

Py. I have, if you are lawyer Jennison.

Jen. I am.

Miss W. If you wish to entertain such company, I'll retire.

Py. Thank you, Miss Wyckoff, you are quite considerate. [*Bowing her out.*

Jen. Be seated, Mr.—

Py. Pymaker—Benjamin Franklin Pymaker—*genus*, printer—*species*, tramp.   [*They sit.*

Jen. Now, Mr. Pymaker, state your business.

Py. First let me hand you this V. Then I may consider you my attorney.   [*Hands it.*

Jen. Thank you. Now proceed.

Py. On the evening of the 9th I was in the woods just south of the village. My meditations were interrupted by the separate entrance of two men, whom I soon spotted as rascals. I took refuge behind a rock, leaving behind me that spoon of Miss Wyckoff's. Villain No. 1 found it and put it into his pocket. Villain No. 2 then appeared and they entered into a confidential confab, which I could not hear, except by snatches. I was confident that they were planning mischief, but, as I had just been banished from the corporation by the marshal, I did not deem it prudent to risk my precious person back in the village to interfere with plans that I knew nothing about. So I tramped on. Here ends chapter one.

Jen. Quite entertaining. Give us chapter two.

Py. After tramping about the country a while, I felt conscience-smitten and determined to come back and find out what their deviltry was. No sooner had I arrived in the village than I learned of the murder and the robbery, both of which occurred on the very night after my forest adventure. I understand that a reward of $2,000 is offered in the first case and $300 in the other.

Jen. You are right—go on.

Py. Well, it's the $2,000 I'm after—can't afford to work for a paltry $300.

Jen. [*Eagerly.*] Have you any clue to the murderer?

Py. I'm on the track of a rascal and I'm going to make a murderer of him if I can, because it's the most profitable just now. But you interrupt the continuity of my narrative. Having got on a big drunk yesterday, I was locked up. This morning I met a fellow prisoner by the name of Hotaling. At the very first his voice and form seemed strangely familiar, but when he spoke of finding a spoon in the woods one evening, marked "J. G. W.," I spotted him as Villain No. 1.

Jen. Do you really think he had any connection with the murder of Mr. Jeffreys?

Py. That's just what I want you to help me figure out.

Jen. Perhaps I have a clue that connects him directly with that affair.

Py. Have you? Then we can work together like a yoke of oxen on this job. But, remember, you are my attorney.

Jen. Never fear—you shall have the reward, if we win it. Take back this bill, too. [*Handing it.*] I need no retainer to interest me in this case, and you need it to buy you a new coat.

Py. Thank you—you are very kind.

Jen. Now the question is, Who is the other villain?

Py. Hold on a minute. This Hotaling wanted me to take a note to Mr. Richard Jeffreys—

Jen. Just as I mistrusted. They're the two villains.

Py. Well, perhaps you know more about this case than I do?

Jen. Did you take that note?

Py. Of course I did, in hopes of getting a glimpse of Villain No. 2.

Jen. Have you delivered it?

Py. No—I've got it here, but the more I read it the less I understand it. Here it is. [*Handing it.*] This ends chapter two. The third chapter will contain the *denouement*, and must be the joint product of our two heads.

Jen. This word "doc" is doubtless an abbreviation of the word "document," and I think I know to what it refers; but this "masquerade in the chimney" puzzles me.

Py. That refers to the disguise worn by the murderer.

Jen. Very likely.

Py. It has already been discovered by Mrs. O'Blarney.

Jen. [*Rising.*] Then I will go and secure those things at once. You had better deliver this note to Mr. Jeffreys and see if you can identify him as Villain No. 2, as you call him. We must work this case up at once. [*Exeunt* L.

SCENE IV.—*Back room in* JEFFREYS' *house.*

Enter MRS. HOUGH, R. H., *with a pan of potatoes.*

Mrs. H. Pompey.

Pomp. [*Within* L.] Dat's de name I goes by.

Mrs. H. Bring me a chair an' knife. I'll pare my potatoes here, where it's cool.

Enter POMPEY *with chair and knife.*

Pomp. Heah am de articles in question.

Mrs. H. [*Sitting* R. H.] There now. I do wonder what's come over Richard now-a-days. He aint half as lively an' sociable as he used to be, an' he keeps himself shut up in his room, for all the world like an oyster in his shell. But I spose his uncle's death goes hard with him. Richard was a wild boy, but I guess he loved his poor old uncle after all, an' feels sorry now for the trouble he made him.

Pomp. Praps he's 'fraid de debble's comin' after him sum nite, too.

Mrs. H. Now, Pompey, do you reelly believe you saw old Satan himself?

Pomp. Didn't I swar to it on de inquest? D'ye spose I'd lie 'bout a sollum ting like dat? 'Pears to me you tink I'se a mitey big liar.

Mrs. H. I thought you might a bin mistaken.

Pomp. Mistaken? Don' de debble go a hoofin it round de country a lookin' fur sumbody to chaw up? An' didn't he mos' chaw me up dat nite?

Mrs. H. Well, Pompey, did you know Miss Nellie's going away to-morrow? I'm 'fraid this will be a lonesome old house when she's gone.

Pomp. Miss Nellie gwine away? Den dis niggah's gwine to pack his Sarytogy an' go too.   [*A loud knock is heard* C. E.

Mrs. H. Go to the door, Pompey.

Pomp. [*Opening door.*] G'way frum heah, white trash! We don' 'low no tramps round heah, no how.

Py. [*Outside.*] I want to see Mr. Richard Jeffreys.

Mrs. H. [*Starting up.*] Good Lord! I know that voice. It's the same tramp I sot the dog on last week. [*Goes to door.*] Go 'way, you ornery scamp, or I'll set the dog on you agin.

Py. I tell you I must see Mr. Jeffreys.

Enter NELLIE L.

Nel. Mrs. Hough—Pompey—what is all this disturbance about?

Pomp. Dare's a doggoned ole white tramp out dare dat says he wants to see Mr. Jeffreys.

Mrs. H. The very same one I sot the dog on last week.

Nel. Pompey, go and call Mr. Jeffreys. [*Exit* POMPEY. *To* PY-MAKER.] Come in, sir, I have sent for Mr. Jeffreys.

Enter PYMAKER.

Py. Thank you, Miss. [*Bowing respectfully.*] I met an old acquaintance of his this morning and he sent a note to him by me.

Mrs. H. [*Aside.*] A likely story! He came to see where Mr. Jeffreys keeps his money.

Enter RICHARD *and* POMPEY.

Rich. Do you wish to see me, sir?

Py. Yes, sir. I met a man this morning by the name of Hotaling, [RICHARD *starts.*] who requested me to hand you this note.

Rich. Follow me, sir.

Py. [*Aside.*] Villain No. 2, as I'm a sinner! [*Exeunt L.*

Mrs. H. It will be lonesome here, Nellie, when you and your father are gone. I wish I could go with you, you have always been so good to me.

Pomp. Aint you gwine to take dis niggah 'long, too?

Nel. It is impossible, though I am sorry to leave you, for you have both been very kind to me. But I am poor now, and I must be my own housekeeper and my own servant. I must work and save to make my poor father comfortable.

Mrs. H. Spoken like the noble girl you are, Nellie. It was a sad night's work that took Mr. Jeffreys from us, made a wreck of your poor old father an' drove you both from this house, an' I know the Lords blessin' will never rest on this house again, until the villain that murdered Mr. Jeffreys is brought to justice. I wish I could do something for you, Nellie, an' your father, too, who always had a smile an' a kind word for me. But I will pray for you both.

Pomp. [*Wiping eyes.*] So will I, too, Miss Nellie—'deed I will.

Nel. God bless you both.

TABLEAU.

END OF ACT IV.

ACT V.

SCENE 1. O'BLARNEY'S *place, as in Act III.* MRS. O'BLARNEY *and* MICHEL *seated at table with glasses of liquor before them.*

Mrs. O'B. Fwat was it, Michel, Mr. Jennison tould yez about the divil's shkin an' the payper?

Mich. Whin he took 'em, he sed Mr. Jeffreys would be loikely to cum afther 'em both, but not a wurd must we shpake till him about ayther one—not fur the loife uv us.

Mrs. O'B. It's divil a word will he git out o' Bridget O'Blarney about 'em—the dhirty thafe that he is, a thryin' to shtale Miss Nellie's property.

Enter RICHARD, 1 L. E., *followed by* PYMAKER.

Rich. Where's Jack Hot-ling's room ?

Mich. In the cownty jale, Mr. Jeffreys—that's where he's a bord in' now.

Py. [*Aside.*] Next door to mine.

Rich. I mean the room he slept in here, you blockhead.

Mich. (*Pointing.*) That's it in there. (RICHARD *goes in.*) Rummige aroun' all ye wants, but divil a soight'll ye git o' what yer afther. Cum, Mr Pymaker, an' take a dhrop wid us, whoile that fool hunts till his hart's contint.   (*They sit and sip liquor.*

Mrs. O'B. An' Mr. Hotaling didn't shtale Miss Wyckoff's shpoons afther ail, Mr. Pymaker ?

Py. Not a bit of it—he found the one he had in the woods.

Mich Thin I've lost me reward an' I can't pay yez fur the cow at all, at all.

Py. Never mind, O'Blarney, you're entitled to a share of the other reward.

Mich. Indade an' thin I will pay yez, mither.

Mss. O'B. I always knew ye would, Michel, fur she was a shwate baste. (*Noise within*) Hear that blackguard a bumpin' aroun' in there now (*Loud crash.*) Oh, the dhirty baste! he's broke me wash bowl an' pitcher.   (*Rushes in.* MICHEL *starts to follow.*

Py. (*Stopping him.*) Hold on—let your mother fix him. There's blood in her eye.

Mrs. O'B. (*Within.*) Git out o' here, ye shtinkin' brute. (*He runs in, followed by her with the broom.*) If iver ye shtick yer hed intil that room agin, I'll larrup yer dhirty back till ther aint a hole bone left in yer ould shkiliton—moind that now.

Rich. (*To* MICHEL.) Where's that paper Hotaling left in his room ?

Mich. Indade an' I niver knew Mr. Hotaling iver had enny payper. Was it a *Fray Press*, a *Posht*, an *Avenin' Nooze*—

Rich. It was a written paper, you fool.

Mich. Faith an' I niver knew afore that they iver printed paypers in wroightin'.

Rich. (*Savagely.*) Who's been in that room ?

Mich. Yersilf an' me ould mither.

Rich. (*Fiercely.*) Who went in there before she did ?

Mich. An' wasn't it yer own silf, Mr. Jeffreys ?

Rich. (*Approaching him threateningly.*) Look here, scoundrel, some one has been in that room and taken something out.

Mrs. O'B. (*Approaching him and flourishing broom.*) I wint in that room, Mr. Jeffreys, an' took a dhirty blackguard out.

Rich. Curse it! I only waste time in parleying with these fools.

           (*Exit* 1 L. E.

Py. He's entirely welcome to all the information he got out of you, O Blarney.

Mich. So he is, an' if the poor divil wasn't in throuble enuff' already, Michel O'Blarney's two fishts'd tache the loike's o' him better'n to call an honesht boy a schoundrel.

Py. Wed, I'll go and find Mr. Jennison.   (*Exit* 1 L. E.

Mrs. O'B. Cum, Michel, we'll go an' git dinner now.

[*Exeunt* 1 R. E.

SCENE II.—*Street.*

Enter JENNISON, PYMAKER and OFFICER, L. H.

Jen. [*To* OFFICER.] I want Hotaling brought down by three o'clock. My intention is to confront Jeffreys with all the witnesses and proofs, at the time of his arrest. My object is to show him that we are acquainted with all the details of his villainy, and that he has no chance of escape. The only safe way for us is to overwhelm him at once with the full force of our evidence. He is shrewd, fearless and self-possessed. Give him but a moment to collect himself and his wealth and influence may enable him to lead us a weary chase before we bring him to justice. You had better put Hotaling in charge of some trusty deputy, so that you may be at liberty to go with me into Jeffreys' office. I may need your assistance before the others come in. Do you understand me fully?

Off. I think I do, and I will see that all is done as you wish.

Jen. Perhaps you had better have Hotaling brought from the jail in a close conveyance of some kind, so as to attract as little attention as possible. I wish to keep the whole affair very quiet, until all is accomplished.

Off. Very well. I will go now and attend to it.   (*Exit* R.

Jen. I believe everything is arranged now. Mrs. O'Blarney and Michel understand all, I suppose?

Py. Have no fears of them. That Michel is as shrewd a young Irishman as I ever met. It would have done your heart good to see how he staved off Jeffreys' inquiries about the will.

Jen. You were there, then?

Py. Yes, I followed Jeffreys right down there. He pointed for O'Blarney's as soon as he read the note, cursing and swearing all the way.

Jen. [*Meditating.*] Mr. Jeffreys was murdered just one week ago to-night, though it seems a month to me—so much has transpired within the interval. The first weekly return of the fatal day seems a fitting time for the unearthing of the villainy and the conviction of the criminal.

Py. Say, Mr. Jennison, just consult your watch and see if it isn't about dinner time. My time-piece (*Putting hand on stomach.*) says it's somewhat past that interesting period.

Jen. (*Looking at watch.*) Past two o'clock! We can't stop for dinner.

Py. Not stop for dinner! That'll do for a man to say, who has

been accustomed to stowing away three square meals a day with un-
flinching regularity, but with me it's another thing al-to-gether.
Lord Byron says:

> —All human history attests,
> That happiness for man—the hungry sinner!—
> Since Eve ate apples, much depends on dinner.

So, in all your future practice, if you want a good-natured, accommodating witness, who will swear to the line, let the truth strike
where it will, look to it that he has a "fair round belly with good
capon lined."

Jen. Come, we'll step into the nearest restaurant.
Py. (*Aside.*) How is that for "special pleading?"   (*Exeunt* R.

SCENE III.—JEFFREYS' *room as in Act I.* RICHARD *discovered in
great excitement.*

Rich. Curse him for the mess he has made of it! Why didn't
he bring me that will instead of letting his infernal greed run away
with him? Why did he make such a blundering fool of himself as
to leave the will where some prying eye has found it? Why was
he so senseless as to hang around her, until the officers got their
clutches upon him? Curse the luck! and yet I may thank myself
for it. If I had only done the work myself, I shouldn't have had
his miserable blunders to harass me now. But why do I stand here
cursing and raving over the *past?* That cannot avail me—I must
grapple sternly with the *present* and determine at once what must
be done. I am liable to be confronted with that will at any moment
—but I will contest it to the bitter end, on the ground of insanity
and undue influence. Nellie and her lover will have a fine time of
getting it allowed. If I can't beat them in the long run, with all
these resources at my command, my name is not Richard Jeffreys.
All is not lost, by any means. But I must see what I can do to get
Hotaling out of his scrape. Then he must leave this vicinity *at
once* or, by heavens! I'll find some means of putting him out of my
way forever. [*A rap is heard* L. H] Come in.

Enter MISS WYCKOFF.

Miss W. Good afternoon, Mr. Jeffreys.
Rich. Good afternoon. Be seated.   [*They sit.*
Miss W. I came to see what success you had with that letter.
Rich. None at all—she's too sharp for us both. Besides you made
a blundering mess of that letter by omitting the date. Any fool
ought to know that a lawyer wouldn't be as careless as that.
Miss W. And yet you were not sharp enough to notice that
omission when you read the letter.
Rich. I was so pleased at your successful imitation of his hand-
writing that I overlooked it. But it is too late now—she is going

to-morrow, bag and baggage, and I can't say I'm sorry, I've got enough to do to manage my property without thinking of matrimony. You'll have to manage your own case with Mr. Jennison.

Miss W. Well, if *your* grapes are sour, *mine* are not.

Enter JENNISON *and* OFFICER L, *the latter passing quietly behind* RICHARD.

Rich. [*Starting up.*] Edward Jennison, you here? Did I not warn you once never to set your foot inside of my house again?

Jen. I remember some such warning—but it was given before the house was yours.

Rich. More of your cursed quibbling? Then I repeat and confirm it now, when the house *is* mine?

Jen. I beg your pardon, Mr. Jeffreys, but the house is *not* yours now.

Rich. What impudence is this? Leave this house instantly or I will have you kicked into the street, like the cur that you are.

Jen. Allow me to escort you from the room, Miss Wyckoff.

Miss W. No, thank you, I will remain.

Rich. Did you hear me? Leave this house at once.

Jen. I appear here, Mr. Jeffreys, as the attorney of Miss Nellie Halliday, who is the sole and lawful owner of these premises, by virtue of the last will and testament of Samuel Jeffreys, your uncle.

Rich. You lie! he never made a will.

Jen. I have it here, [*Showing it.*] duly executed—

Rich. It is a forgery! and your attempt to foist it upon the public will not succeed. You thought to secure a portion of my uncle's wealth by marrying Nellie Halliday; and now since he has not left her a cent, you have adopted this plan of getting the whole. Edward Jennison, you are a bare-faced scoundrel. Leave this house or I will use force.   [*Rushes at* JENNISON.

Off. [*Seizing him.*] You are my prisoner, sir.

Rich. [*Starting back.*] For what?

Off. Be patient a moment and you will learn.

Rich. Who is my accuser?

Jen. I am. First I accuse you of the theft and concealment of the last will and testament of Samuel Jeffreys, late deceased. That will, which I now hold in my hand—with the exception of a legacy to be paid to you and another to George Halliday—vests the title of all the property of Samuel Jeffreys—both real and personal—in Miss Nellie Halliday.

Miss W. Nellie Halliday the owner of all this property!

Rich. I tell you no such will was ever made!

Jen. Richard Jeffreys, I also accuse you of the murder of your uncle, Samuel Jeffreys.

Miss W. Murder!—Richard Jeffreys!

Rich. [*Furiously.*] You lie! Your life shall answer for this insult!
        [*Rushes savagely at* JENNISON.

Off. [*Forcing him back.*] Be quiet! Another such move and I'll put the irons on you.

Rich. [*Wild with fury*] He lies! he cannot bring the proofs.

Jen. That I may tell my story better, I'll confirm it with witnesses and proofs. [*Rings bell.*

Enter MRS. O'BLARNEY *and* MICHEL *with a bundle,* PYMAKER *and* POMPEY, HOTALING *handcuffed and in charge of an officer, and* NELLIE.

Rich. Is my house to be filled with this rabble? Edward Jennison, you shall pay dearly for this.

Jen. Let me remind you that this is *not* your house. Here is the owner herself, to grant this rabble her permission to stay.

Rich. You here, Hotaling?

Hot. Unfortunately I am.

Jen. Yes, Richard Jeffreys, your companion in crime has been arrested for his complicity in that foul murder and now stands in irons before you.

Rich. [*Aside.*] I'll face it through—he's trying to frighten me into a confession. [*Aloud.*] Really, Mr Jennison, I'm getting deeply interested in your little farce. Play it through—but remember my turn comes next—a tragedy instead of a comedy.

Jen. On the night of the 9th you met Jack Hotaling in the woods just south of the village, and then and there plotted the death of your uncle and the theft of the will. Mr. Pymaker was a witness to that interview and he is now able to identify you both.

Py. I can do that little thing gentlemen.

Rich. [*Aside.*] Hell furies!

Jen. Just before your appearance Mr. Pymaker dropped this silver spoon, [*Showing it.*] marked "J. G. W.," which Hotaling picked up, and which was found upon his person when he was arrested for burglary,

Hot. [*To Pymaker.*] And you knew this all the time?

Py. Yes, I was the "picnic party" that lost the spoon—though my rations were far from being of a picnic quality.

Rich. And how did you come by that spoon, fellow?

Miss W. He stole it from my house one day when my cook was kind enough to give him a lunch in the kitchen—

Py. And you were unkind enough to hustle me out unceremoniously, so I took the spoon in revenge.

Rich. [*Sneering.*] Is it by the testimony of this thief that you expect to convict me of murder? Go on, you have made a very fine beginning indeed.

Jen. This morning Mr Pymaker delivered you a note from Jack Hotaling, telling you where the will could be found—

Rich. Did you read that note, scoundrel?

Py. I so far violated the confidence reposed in me, Mr. Jeffreys.

Rich. An honorable witness you have, indeed. A few more such admissions on his part will help your case amazingly.

Py. This last admission has wiped out the effect of the other concerning the theft of the spoon, for there's "honor among thieves." Now my conduct in reading that note shows there's no honor in me. *Ergo*, I am *not* a thief.

Rich. Your character and your logic are on a par.

Jen. You took advantage of your uncle's strange delusion. At your instigation, Jack Hotaling. disguised as Satan—a fitting disguise for heinous a crime—strangled the poor old man in his bed.

Rich. [*Aside.*] Curse him! how he is hemming me in.

Pomp. [*To* HOTALING.] An' was you dat ar debble?

Hot. Silence!

Pomp. Now I know you was—dat's jis wat de debble tole me dat ar nite.

Rich. Keep your mouth shut, Hotaling.

Jen. Yesterday morning Mrs. O'Blarney found something in Hotaling's room, that is of considerable importance in this case. Let us see it, Michel.

Mich. [*Opening bundle.*] Indade an' here it is, Mr. Jennison—the ould divil's shkin—harns, tail an' all.

Rich. [*Staggering back.*] Damnation!

Mrs. O'B. The very same that I found in the ould chimney.

Jen. One thing more.

Rich. [*Aside.*] For God's sake what's coming next?

Jen. This knife, marked on the handle with the letter "H.," was found beneath the window from which Hotaling leaped in his escape from the house. It is identified as one that Jack Hotaling told Michel O'Blarney had been presented to him by a friend.

Mich. It's the very same knoife—I'd know it among tin thousand.

Enter MRS. HOUGH, L. H., *in great agitation.*

Mrs. H. What do I hear? Richard Jeffreys murdered his poor old uncle?—my Richard whom I have so often carried in my arms? I will not believe it. [*Going to him.*] Richard, I know you have been wayward and wilful, but I cannot believe you are a murderer. Tell me it is not so. [*Richard turns away.*] He turns away. Oh God! can it be true?

Nel. [*Leading her away.*] It is an awful charge, Mrs. Hough, but we fear it is too true.

Jen. Richard Jeffreys, in view of all these circumstances, I again accuse of the murder of your uncle on the night of the 10th of August. Officer, do your duty. [OFFICER *starts to arrest him.*]

Rich. Back, back! (*Draws knife and stabs himself.*) Ha, ha, ha! Edward Jennison, you shall never triumph over me in a felon's cell. I shall soon be beyond your reach. (*Falls into* OFFICER'S *arms.*

Mrs. H. (*Kneeling by him and bending over him.*) Oh, Richard! was it for this that I watched over you after your dying mother left you to my care? My heart is broken and my gray hairs will soon follow you to the grave.

Rich. Nellie Halliday, take Edward Jennison for your husband. Lavish upon him that wealth which you so artfully induced my

uncle to leave you.   But remember, with every dollar of it goes a
dying man's curse. You have won her, Edward Jennison, but I
fought you to the last—   (*Faints*

Mrs. H. Oh, my poor boy is dying !   (*Wringing hands.*
Rich. (*Struggling to his feet.*)   Die ? Who said die ? I must not
die unforgiven, with all this load of sin to drag me down—and yet
—oh God !—I'm growing weaker—I cannot—(*Sinks to floor and dies.*

Enter HALLIDAY, C. E., *coming down front.*

Nel. (*Starting toward father.*) Oh, father—

[*He passes down front to where* RICHARD *lies, with* MRS. HOUGH *bending over him, and stands* C., *pointing at him.*

Hal. Richard Jeffreys, thy crimes have found thee out. But one
short week hast thou enjoyed that wealth for which thou didst bar-
ter thy soul. And now thou diest, adding self-murder to thy long
list of crimes. When the grave shall have received thy mortal
frame, and thine immortal spirit shall have returned, for judgment,
unto him who gave it, then shall man inscribe upon thy tomb

HERE LIES

THE LAST OF THE HOUSE OF JEFFREYS.

TABLEAU.

.THE END.

www.ingramcontent.com/pod-product-compliance
Lightning Source LLC
Chambersburg PA
CBHW030903260626
47169CB00008B/2661